Skeeter
Night Howler's MC
New Orleans
Book 2
Marissa Ann

Table of Contents

Author's Note

I plan to expand into many other genres over the next couple of years but unlike so many of my fellow Author's, I do not plan to change my pen name to separate those titles from each other.

While I am moving into other genres, I do not plan to stop writing several Motorcycle Club titles as I have been doing each year.

Thank you all for your continued support of my titles.

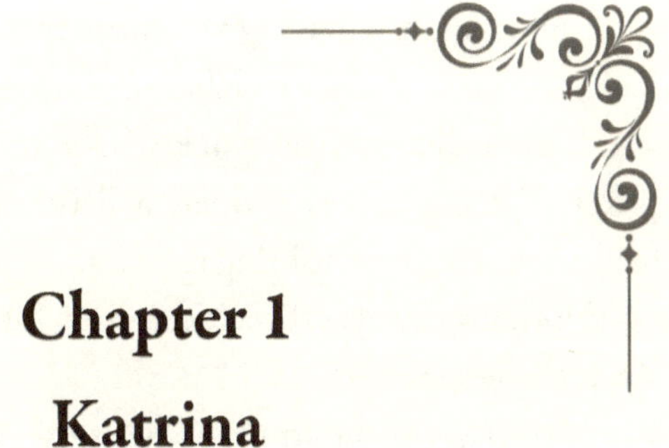

Chapter 1
Katrina

"Ma'am? Can you open your eyes?" I hear from a voice that sounds so far away.

Trying to turn my head in the direction it's coming from, pain shoots through every fiber of my body. A groan escapes my lips, surprising me with the sound.

"Water?" I barely say above a whisper. My throat feels impossibly dry.

I feel cold fingers on my face just as one of my eyes is forced open and a bright light invades the darkness.

I jump, trying to turn away which causes even more pain through my skull.

"Please." I beg, not knowing if these people are trying to hurt me.

"Give her some water!" I hear a growly voice command from somewhere else in the room.

I force my own eyes open, looking for the source of the voice. Everything is fuzzy and blurry.

"Here." I hear the voice yet again but much closer. Almost too close.

I jump slightly feeling yet another touch to the side of my face just before a straw touches my bottom lip.

"Drink. But not too quickly." The voice somehow becomes softer. Forcing my eyes open a little more, I make out the features of the man holding the cup.

Noticing my eyes directed at him, he stares back as I slowly sip at the water.

Letting go of the straw, he pulls the cup away.

"Thank you." I whisper, closing my eyes once more.

"You are welcome, Katrina." He says back but my eyes pop back open.

"Who are you?" I ask.

Smirking slightly, "I'm called Skeeter."

Thinking it over for several long seconds, I reply, "What kind of name is that?"

He only chuckles back in answer.

Looking slowly around the room, I notice what must be a doctor and several nurses in the room.

"Why am I in the hospital?" Looking down at my own arms I realize they are covered in bruises. "Was I in an accident?"

Looking up I see confusion on all their faces. My heart begins to pound at the fact no one is saying anything.

"Can you tell us what your last name is, Miss Katrina?" The doctor asks, moving closer to the bed.

Thinking about his question I realize that I don't remember what it is. I'm actually not certain Katrina is my name either.

"I...um, I'm not sure." Tears invade my eyes. The guy next to the bed puts his hand into mine, barely squeezing my fingers.

"It's okay. There's plenty of time for you to remember everything. For now its best if you rest for a while." The doctor states, writing on the tablet in his hand. "I'll be back to check on you before my shift ends." He smiles, glancing over at Skeeter before walking out the door.

"I should let you rest too." Skeeter says, letting go of my hand.

"You'll come back?" I ask, almost in a panic at the thought of him not being here.

"I won't be far." He smiles back at me before slowly closing the door behind him.

Laying back into my pillow, I struggle to keep my eyes open and realize the nurse must have put something into my IV before leaving with the doctor.

Why can't I remember? I think to myself before falling back to sleep.

Skeeter

"She still doesn't remember anything. Not even her own name. Were you able to at least find a last name for her?" Doc asks outside of Katrina's room.

Watching her through the glass window, I can only shake my head in answer. I come by every day to check on her and to talk with her doctor about her condition.

"Do you think she'll ever regain her memory?" I ask.

"It's hard to say." He shrugs. "The brain is a complex organ that we still don't fully understand."

"It may be best that she doesn't remember. At least whatever part of her life she was in that hell."

"Can't say that I don't agree with you there. I may not know the details but I see her medical charts. She's had broken bones that are healed now but I can tell she never got medical treatment because of how they grew back." He answers. "I have other patients to check on. I'll be back around later before the end of my shift."

"Thank you doctor." I shake his hand before he walks away.

Turning towards her door, I knock gently before pushing it open further.

"Hey you." I greet her with a grin.

"Hey." She answers. The wild eyed look that seems to always be on her face is still present.

"How are you feeling today?" I ask, taking a seat next to the bed.

"I'm okay. The doctor said that I should be able to leave soon." She says softly, looking down at her hands that are twisting the sheet.

"Well that's a good thing right?"

"I guess so." She answers but before I can say anything else her door opens with a nurse coming in.

"Are you ready for your shower?" The nurse asks with a smile.

Katrina looks over at me expectantly.

"Get you a shower. I'll stop back by later." I smile, patting her on the hand and walking out the door.

I have to get back to the clubhouse and make sure my guys got the last set of girls moved into their new homes across the city.

Some of the girls we saved from that warehouse had family that they went back to. But there were still some left that had nowhere to go so the club opened up several of the houses that we had bought in the last year to use as safe houses.

We are even helping them with getting jobs. At least for those who are not so traumatized that they can't work. The ones that needed therapy are getting that as well after I called in a favor.

The feds we were working with are on our asses about where the women are at because only a select few know. I may have allowed our club to work with them but that doesn't mean we trust them. Far from it.

Back at the clubhouse I find Animal, one of the newest club brothers in the main room.

"The women get settled in okay?" I ask him.

"Yeah. Buzz said he'd check in with you later today once he had his sister settled in at his place." He answers.

There's something about Animal that I just haven't ever liked. I've been unable to pinpoint what it is. Something in his eyes maybe that I don't fully trust.

"Thanks. I'll be in my office for a while before I head back to the hospital this afternoon."

"That girl going to be released soon?" His question has me stopping to turn back in his direction.

"There a reason you're asking?" I ask calmly.

Shrugging his shoulders, he says, "Just wondering if she'll need a place at one of the houses."

"I'll let you know." I answer quickly, walking away.

Shutting the door to my office, I pull my phone from my pocket and dial Buzz's number.

"Prez." He answers quickly.

"Thought I'd check in on your sister. How she doing?" I ask.

"She's alright. A little jumpy but I think with time she'll heal."

"She always was a strong one." I smile remembering her younger self.

"Yeah. Did you need something else?" He asks knowing me too well.

"Not really."

He starts laughing in my ear. "I know you man. Talk to me. You have something on your mind that is heavy enough that you called me only to hold the phone like some chick."

"You are an asshole." I growl.

"But I'm an asshole that's right." He laughs again. "So out with it."

"Something about Animal tells me to not trust him."

"He's one of our brothers." He states. "You didn't object when we voted him in."

"It's probably just my imagination." I sigh, rubbing my forehead.

"That is highly unlikely. I'll see what I can dig up." He says.

"Thanks man."

"No problem, Prez." He says as we hang up.

He's right though. Usually when my gut is telling me something is off, it normally is.

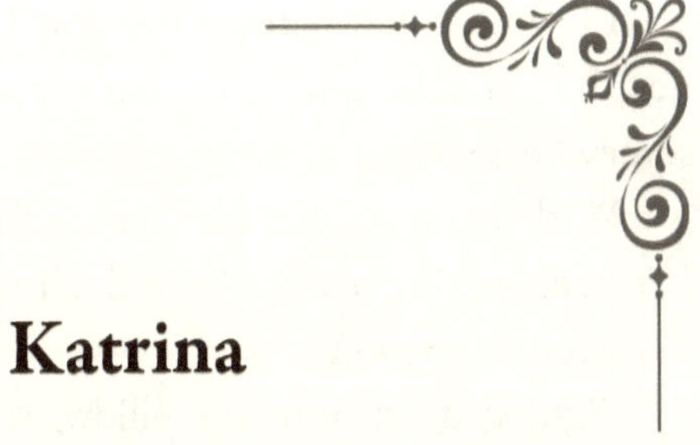

Katrina

Looking at myself in the mirror, I don't recognize my face and it's not from all the bruises that are slowly fading away.

I've asked myself numerous times, who are you, only to always come back with the exact same answer. I don't know.

Surely I had a life before this happened to me? Although I can't remember it. I can't even remember what exactly happened to me. Not that anyone has given me the whole story.

Even Skeeter has stayed quiet about some of the details that I know for a fact he knows. He's always so nice about telling me that if I can't remember then it's probably best that no one else tells me either.

Somehow I feel like that isn't the type of person that I am though. I want to know, even if I can't remember it.

The doctor said that I would be released soon but where the hell am I going to go? I can't remember if I have family or not that would take me in.

Sighing heavily I look at myself once more in the mirror.

"I don't know who you are but I am determined to make it." I tell myself with a firm shake of my head.

I'll find somewhere to live and I'll get a job. I'll make a new life, at least until I can remember if I already have one somewhere else.

With a new resolve, I head back to my hospital bed. While I've been getting better, I'm still a little weak in the legs when I've been up too long.

Sighing down into my pillow, I fall asleep wondering if Skeeter will once again be there in the morning when I wake up.

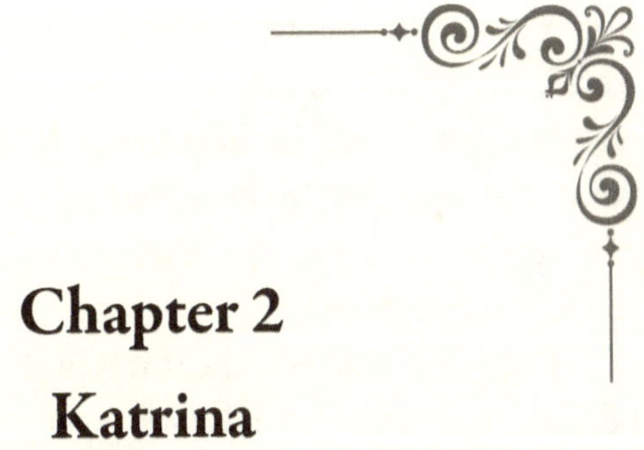

Chapter 2
Katrina

I'm sitting on the side of my hospital bed when the doctor and nurse come in. With a smile, she begins to take all my vitals as he looks over my chart in his hand.

"How are you feeling today?" He asks, finally looking up at me.

"A whole lot better actually. I didn't have to call the night nurses to help me with getting to the bathroom." I answer with a small smile.

"That's really good. Everything seems to be mending just fine which is why I'm in here right now. I think you are well enough to be released."

"Great." my smile falters.

"It's my understanding that you don't really have anywhere to go once you leave here. Is that right?"

"I guess you could say that." My hands start twisting the sheet in my hands.

"I think it would be a great idea if you allowed me to put you into the inpatient therapy program." He walks over, taking a seat in the chair closest to me.

"What's the inpatient therapy program?" I look at him, wondering what he means.

"You would still be here in the hospital, just on another floor. That way you have somewhere safe to stay while still getting the treatment and therapy you'll need with all that you've been through."

His sincere look tells me this is probably my best option so I don't exactly know what is keeping me from agreeing just yet.

"If you agree to this, I would just need you to sign these forms here." He hands over a stack of papers.

Looking down at the papers in my hand, I look back at him for a second and he then hands me a pen.

Taking the pen, I hold it over the first page, ready to sign before I stop myself.

"If it's okay. Can I have a little while to think about it?" I ask. Wanting time to talk with the only person I have felt was trustworthy since waking up here a little more than a week ago.

"Sure. I'll be back around later today." His smile is brief as they both walk back out of the room.

Once they are both gone, I pick up the stack of papers in front of me and sit back to read them over. I need to be absolutely certain of these documents before I sign them.

Somehow, I know exactly what all the legal jargon on these papers means which just adds to all the questions that have started to pile up inside of my head.

Maybe I worked in a courthouse or something before?

An hour later, I'm finished reading over all the documents and I'm pissed. This doctor wants to admit me to the mental facility on the top floor with no way to sign myself out at a later date.

I'm up pushing the button for the nurse and demanding to see the doctor again before I can think it over.

Soon as the door opens, I spin around to let loose on him but its Skeeter coming through the door.

"Are you okay? What's wrong?" He says, coming further into the room.

"I want to be released. Today! Right this minute!" I rush my words.

"I thought you were? The nurse I spoke to on the phone a little while ago said the doctor planned to release you so I came here to give you a ride."

Walking over to the bed, I pick up the stack of papers and shove them into his hand.

"He wants to stick me into the mental facility upstairs!" My outburst has his brows raising high on his forehead.

"Why the fuck would he want that?" Skeeter growls.

"I don't know. I want to leave. Right now!" I stomp my foot a little and the side of his mouth quirks up at me. If his look didn't look so sexy I'd probably slap him.

"Give me a few minutes to go talk to the doctor and get your release papers. Alright? Then we'll go." He walks towards the door.

"But go where?" I say to the empty room. I really don't care where. I just know I'm not staying in this hospital a moment longer.

Skeeter

Balling the papers Katrina handed me in my hand, I try to maintain control of my anger. Why the fuck would the doctor ask this of her is beyond me.

Walking up to the nurse's desk, I put on my best smile for the cute little nurse behind the desk.

"Hey doll, the doctor said that Katrina could be released today. Can you see about starting her discharge papers for me?"

"Sure. Just give me a few minutes to find the file." She grins back, twirling a strand of her hair.

Turning back around, I take my phone from my pocket and text Animal letting him know Katrina will be staying at the safe house that is only a few blocks away from the clubhouse.

He texts back immediately asking if I need him to take her and I let him know that I will do it myself. He doesn't need to know that I'm also doing it so that I know exactly what room she is in.

"I have them ready." The nurse says just as the doctor walks up and my anger bubbles up.

"What the fuck do you mean trying to get her to admit herself to the mental facility without any way of ever getting out?" I crowd his space, my hands once again balled into fists.

"I just thought it was a better alternative." He shoves his nose further into the air.

"Better alternative than what?" My voice is low now. Those who know me would know that it means danger.

"Putting herself into the same situation she found herself in before." His words almost get me to react but I rein it in.

Smiling widely, I step back. "Something deep down tells me that it was an upstanding man such as yourself that got her into that mess. Watch yourself Doc. I'd hate to know you were lost in the Bayou."

Seeing a movement behind the doctor, my eyes collide with Katrina's.

"Can I sign out now?" She asks, holding her back up straight.

"Yes ma'am. Just sign these forms here and you are free to go." The nurse says quickly, looking between me and the doctor.

Once Katrina finishes, I guide her down the hall. Behind us I hear the nurse telling the doctor that he'd best be careful with what enemies he makes in this part of town.

If he knows what's good for him, he'll take her advice.

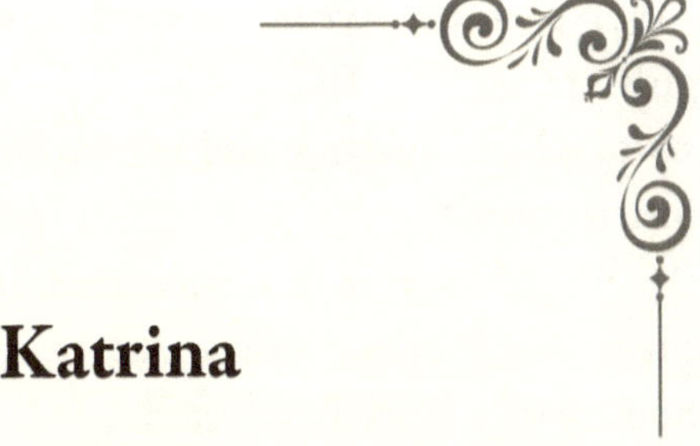

Katrina

Stepping outside of the hospital, I raise my face up to the sun, closing my eyes to soak in its rays. I wonder how long it's been since I was able to do such a thing.

While no one has told me the full details, I know that I was being held somewhere, drugged and beaten.

Opening my eyes, I look over at the man next to me who is just standing there, patient and still as a statue.

"Thank you." I say out loud and his eyes meet my own. He just nods back in understanding.

"I'm parked this way?" He nods in the direction and we head that way.

"Nice truck." I comment once we are next to it.

He shrugs his shoulders, "It's still a cage."

Stopping myself from climbing in, I look at him with raised brows. "A cage?"

"That's what we, the club, calls most vehicles."

"Right. I almost forgot you're in a motorcycle club."

Getting in, he shuts my door before getting in the driver seat.

"So where are we going? I didn't think beyond getting out of that hospital." I feel my face turn red at my admission.

"No worries. We have a safe house where some of the other girls are staying. Thought you'd be okay there for now." He states it like a question and I shake my head before he pulls out into the road.

We mostly ride in silence until I feel the truck turn into a small neighborhood and come to a stop in front of a cute little house with a fenced back yard.

Another woman steps out onto the porch, lighting a cigarette and sitting on the porch swing.

"How many women are here?" I ask quietly.

"You'll be the fifth. Don't worry, you all have your own room. You'll have to share the bathrooms and the kitchen though."

With a shake of my head, I grab the handle, opening the door. Skeeter is out and around to my side before I can shut it.

"You'll be safe here. Not even the feds know where our safe houses are." He says.

Looking over at him, I automatically comment, "You have the houses buried within shell companies."

His head jerks in my direction with surprise.

"How do you know that?" He asks with a serious expression.

"I honestly have no idea." I shrug.

Looking at me for another long moment, we head towards the door. The woman on the porch just watches us but doesn't move or say anything to us.

"Oh, hey Skeeter! What are you doing here?" A younger girl coming down the hall asks.

"Gina, this is Katrina. She's gonna stay for a while. Can you point us toward the empty room?"

"Nice to meet you. It's down this way." We follow her down the hall all the way to the last door.

Walking in, the room is beautiful and smells like lilacs.

"The closet is over here for you to put clothes in." Gina says, pointing to the door.

My face flames remembering that all I have is what is on my back. I have no idea if what I'm wearing is even mine.

"Gina, could you give us a minute?" Skeeter asks and she leaves the room. "Here." He says, handing me an envelope.

"What's this?"

"Everything you'll need for now." He watches as I open it, pulling out a wad of cash.

"I can't take this." I state, shoving it back into the envelope.

"Yes, you can. Every woman here gets the exact same thing to help get her started. There's also a list of places with job openings. Just tell them Skeeter sent you."

"How can they hire me without a driver's license or a birth certificate?"

"It'll be off the books. For now it's the best we can do."

Not wanting to seem ungrateful, I hold the envelope tightly to my chest.

"Thank you. For everything." My eyes cloud up with tears.

"Yep." He nods quickly, looking away. "I'll get Gina to loan you something for tonight and I'll come back tomorrow to take you shopping for the things you need."

I look him over slowly trying to imagine this man in his leather vest standing in the women's underwear while I pick out panties.

The image that creates causes me to snort to hold back a laugh.

"What?" He asks, turning to look at me quickly.

"Nothing. Tomorrow would be great. Thank you again."

"You're gonna need to stop thanking me so much."

"Only when you stop doing things that no longer require it." I grin back at him.

"I'll see you tomorrow." He smiles goodbye and is gone a few seconds later.

Chapter 3
Katrina

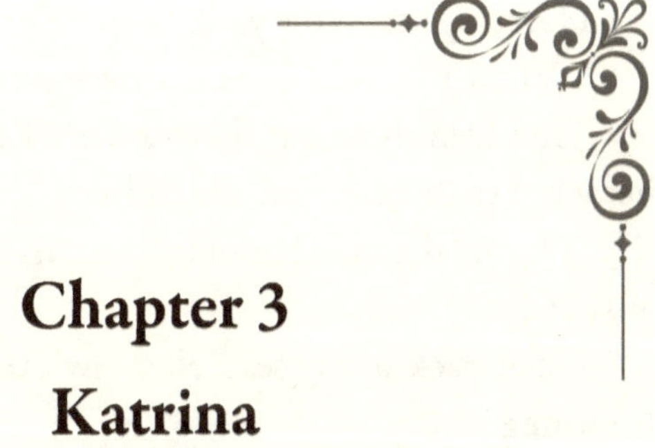

I never thought that when I applied for jobs last week that I'd get a call back so quickly.

I'm excited to finally have a way to make my own money and an excuse to get out of the house.

Some of those girls get down right catty over some of the MC guys that come around often.

I was under the impression that the guys from Skeeter's club were not allowed to date the girls. I don't plan to stick my nose into their business though.

Looking over myself in the mirror one last time, I grab my purse and head out the door to wait for my cab.

"Where you off to?" A rough guy's voice startles me as I come out the door.

Grabbing my heart with one hand, I smile over at where he's sitting on the swing. I can't remember his name though. "To work actually."

Just as I finish speaking, the cab I ordered pulls up at the curb. "Guess I'll see ya." I try to sound more chipper than I am.

"Yep. You will." He grins in a way that makes my skin crawl in a bad way.

Hurrying across the yard, I slip into the back of the cab.

"Where to miss?" The cab driver asks.

"The Den. It's a bar downtown?" I frame it as a question because I can't remember the address.

"I know the one. Shouldn't take us long to get there." He answers.

I lean back in my seat, close my eyes and try to slow my breathing.

My nerves are wound tight, unsure if I can actually do the job these guys have hired me to do.

It's frustrating not knowing what you know how to do and what you don't. "Wish I could remember." I whisper to myself.

I'm so lost in thought about what I may have been doing before I lost my memory that I don't realize that the cab has come to a stop.

"We're here, miss." His voice catches my attention.

Paying him quickly, I get out and walk up to the front door.

"Here we go." I whisper, pulling open the door.

Several hours later, I feel better about accepting this job. Either I've waited tables before or I'm a natural at this job.

The drinks are all super simple to make so there's no learning curve on mix drink concoctions like you see at most other bars.

Most of the clientele seem to be rough looking men but all are friendly.

The women are a tad under-dressed if you ask me but the men they are trying to attract seem to like it a good bit.

They however, are not that friendly.

Twice now I've had to bite my tongue when one of the women cussed me for not being fast enough in her estimation of getting her a beer.

"You don't have to take no one's shit here, you know." Skeeter's voice almost directly behind me makes my stomach flutter.

"What are you doing here?" I turn with a smile only for him.

"Just passing through." He shrugs.

Seeing another guy at the end of the bar trying to get my attention, I look back at Skeeter.

"Don't let me keep you from your duties. I'll be here for a bit." Skeeter smirks, turning away with a new beer in his hand, making me wonder if he stole it from behind the bar.

Surely Skeeter isn't a thief though. He doesn't seem the type to do something so silly.

Getting the drink order, I keep glancing in the direction that Skeeter went.

Seeing him reach the stairs leading to the top floor, he's greeted by my boss and the two men walk up the stairs together.

Almost at the top, he looks back at me once again and winks. I feel my entire face flame hot at being caught watching him.

Turning away quickly, I busy myself with wiping the bar. My hands once again shaking with nerves.

Looking down at them I wonder if I was always this nervous or if it's from the so-called trauma that I can't even remember.

Skeeter has made sure that all the girls in the house have access to a therapist who comes by every couple of days to sit and talk with each of us individually.

She told me that although I don't remember what happened, my body does and will find ways to alert me when something feels out of place.

Are the feelings I get when I look at Skeeter something that is out of place? Out of the ordinary? I really don't know. I'm not scared of him though. Not in the way that the other guy at the house earlier made me feel.

Skeeter says that I can trust all of his men though as if they were him and I trust Skeeter completely.

Skeeter

Sitting down at the table with Cross, I watch as Katrina works the bar down below.

"How's Katrina working out for you?" I ask.

"Pretty good actually. All the guys seem to like her. Can't say the same for the sluts though." He chuckles, drinking his beer.

"Make sure they all know she's off limits." I growl low.

"They know Skeeter. No one's going to mess with that girl. Besides, did you see the tank top I made her wear? I told her it was part of the job attire." He chuckles again and I shake my head at him.

"She doesn't even realize what the emblem is." I shake my head at his antics.

The emblem on the shirt is one that Renee, Pops Ole Lady, designed specifically for women that were part of the club family. Setting them completely apart from the club sluts running around.

"Nope. But at least it protects her from all those bikers down there. Not even the out of state clubs will try to touch her now as long as she's wearing that shirt." He shakes his head firmly.

He definitely has a point but I think that shirt is also part of the reason some of those sluts down there are giving her a hard time. They all try to push the Ole Lady's at first to see what they can get away with.

Katrina is going to have to step up and assert herself. I can't do it for her. They wouldn't respect her as much if I stepped in to handle it. Even if she isn't actually in the club family.

I drink several beers over the next few hours, talking with Cross as I watch her work. She never seems to slow down or ask for breaks.

She even seems to smile while she's working. Her smiles are something I could get used to seeing. They seem to light up her entire face.

She's a very beautiful woman. One that seems to have taken over my thoughts the last week to the point that I woke up with a raging hard on dreaming about the panties that I watched her pick out at the store even though I tried like hell not to see.

Even now, sitting here in this crowd with a club brother across from me, I feel an ache behind my zipper as those pink lacy panties of hers flash in my head.

Moving around to adjust myself without being seen, I turn my eyes back to my beer away from that delectable body down below.

I try to think of something else but all I can come up with is that beautiful blush she gets on her face when I catch her looking at me for too long.

I wonder if I can make her turn that color by fucking her in front of a mirror from behind.

Fuck. If I so much as try to adjust myself now, I'll break my own cock off.

"Earth to Skeeter!" Cross yells, finally getting my attention. "Jesus Christ man! Even I can see the thoughts going through your head!" He laughs out.

"Fuck off!" I growl, turning my beer up and finding it empty already.

"Get me another beer!" I yell over his laughing.

By two a.m. I'm definitely more than ready to leave, having only stayed to keep an eye on Katrina for her first night at work.

Now that I'm here, I might as well give her a ride back to the house. I stopped drinking several hours ago, switching over to club soda, not wanting to get behind the wheel with a lot of alcohol in my system.

"Ready to go?" I ask her, walking up to the bar she's wiping down.

"Almost. Why?" She asks, looking everywhere but at me.

"I'll give you a ride back to the house." I state almost like a demand. Her eyes jump to mine quickly and I soften my expression. It's not her fault that I've had a hard on all night for her.

Not saying anything else to me, she moves to take a load of dishes to the back to be washed. I lean against the bar prepared for her to make me wait but she comes back within a few minutes.

"Okay. I'm ready." She calmly says, putting her purse over her shoulder and walking towards the door expecting me to follow.

I grin in her direction doing exactly that while my eyes eat up how sexy her ass looks in those jeans.

As we walk out the door, I'm not paying attention to anything but the sway of her ass so I'm caught off guard by someone saying my name as soft hands wrap around my upper arm.

"Hi Skeeter, I didn't know you were coming by tonight."

Looking at the woman, I try to remember her name but can't seem to. Instead I stare hard at her for a second and at her hands on my arm until she finally gets the message to let go.

Out of the corner of my eye I can see that Katrina has also stopped walking and is studying the woman who seems to know me.

"Do I know you?" I demand.

She pouts out her lip which is supposed to be sexy. Maybe for some men it is but to me it just looks childish. "I can't believe you don't remember me. We went to school together."

Studying her I finally realize exactly who she is.

"Oh yeah. You're the one that let the entire football team have a piece of her snatch on Prom night." At her gasp, I turn and walk towards Katrina, throwing my arm over her shoulder as we walk.

"That was a little harsh." Katrina peeps up at me.

Shrugging my shoulders, I keep walking. "It was the truth."

As we get to my bike, Katrina stands there and stares as I grab a helmet for her to put on.

"You didn't bring your jeep?" She asks, taking the helmet from my hand.

"I like riding whenever I can. You'll enjoy it. I promise I won't let you fall off." I grin knowing that while she will enjoy the ride, so will I with her body pressed against my back.

I get on first, then extend my hand to help her on, making sure to put her feet on the pegs correctly so she doesn't burn her legs on the pipes.

"Wrap your arms around me and just hold on. When I lean for a turn, you lean with me but not more than I do, okay?"

Starting up the bike, I rev the motor a second and we take off into the night. Her arms wrapping around me even tighter. All I can think about are those huge globes of her pressed into my back as well as her thighs.

Unable to resist the temptation, my left hand reaches down, grabbing her thigh to squeeze it closer to me. Soon I feel her relax into me and begin to enjoy the ride.

Katrina

When we first took off on the bike, I was scared to death so I know that I've never been on a motorcycle before.

It didn't take long though for me to get used to it and be comfortable behind him. Trusting him to keep me safe.

Once I stopped worrying about falling though is when the real trouble starts. The feeling of the bike vibrating seems to go through my entire body.

Especially in the lower region and I become all too aware of his hot body pressed into my front.

His hand on my thigh does nothing but heighten the feelings running through me.

Wiggling slightly to hopefully stop the sensation, my pussy rubs against my own clothes and sends a shock through my core.

I can't hold back the gasp that escapes my lips.

As if he knows what is happening, his hand on my thigh begins to rub my leg. My breathing hitches up further and all I want to do is tilt my pelvis forward into his back.

My hands grab fistfuls of his shirt in the front and I swear I feel him chuckle.

Looking ahead I see that we have finally turned onto my road. I breathe a sigh of relief as we come to a stop in front of the house.

Grabbing my hand he helps me off the bike first before getting off as well. I'm unable to look at him as I fumble with the latch under my chin.

"Here. Let me." He whispers, swatting my hands away that are shaking.

Once the helmet is off, his fingers tilt my chin up until I am looking into his eyes.

"First time on a bike?" He grins that sexy ass grin of his.

I'm still unable to speak so I shake my head instead.

"Glad I was your first." My eyes widen at the statement and he chuckles at me. "Sweet dreams Katrina." He moves slowly making sure of my reaction as he leans closer and kisses me softly right next to my lips before moving away again.

I watch as he climbs back onto the bike.

"You should go inside now." He raises an eyebrow.

Turning away I head towards the door but turn back to him one last time. "Thank you for the ride." He nods back and watches me all the way to the door.

I don't hear the roar of his bike leave until I am all the way inside of the house.

Chapter 4
Skeeter

Sitting at my desk going over paperwork, I yawn for the hundredth time today.

Sitting at the bar almost every night to watch over Katrina as she works so that I can make sure she gets home safely hasn't left me with a lot of hours to sleep.

Being ex-military you'd think I'd be used to it all but that is one thing I always hated.

Looking over at the clock, I see that I have a couple hours left before I should head back to the bar.

I've no idea why I've taken such a keen interest in her almost from the very beginning.

The last few weeks though, that interest has switched to something a little more physical.

I woke up this morning with my cock hard as a damn boulder after dreaming about her looking at me with those soft ass doe eyes.

My soft silk sheets rubbing against me had me bolting for the shower to calm myself down.

Thinking about that dream even now has me almost ready to explode. My phone ringing interrupts my thoughts though.

"Skeeter." I say harshly, recognizing the number.

"How are things?" Agent Fox greets as if he doesn't know that I'm sick of all their shit.

"I'm still not giving you the locations." I lean back in my chair.

"I'm not calling for that, although you may want to check on all the girls you stash somewhere."

"What the fuck you mean by that?" I growl.

"The girls that did go with us? A few of them are missing yet again."

"You sure they just aren't hiding from your superiors?"

If I were them, I'd hide from their asses too if they are hounding those girls like they've tried to hound the ones that decided to go with my club for safety.

"No. One of the girls that was back with her mother came up missing from her own house in the middle of the night."

His answer has me sitting up straighter in my chair.

"How the fuck does that even happen? I thought you fucks kept guards outside?"

"We are short staffed and don't have the manpower to cover each victim."

My fist slams down on my desk at his answer.

"You fuckers promised those girls they'd be safe! What the fuck?" I yell into the phone ready to strangle him.

"Come on Skeeter, you know how it is." He tries to calm me but it's too late for that.

"This is the end of our talks, Agent Fox." I say through clenched teeth.

"Do you seriously want to be on the FBI's radar again? I won't be able to help your club if this is the path you decide to take." He says a few beats later.

"My club will be fine." I smirk even though he can't see me.

"Don't mess up this investigation. I'd hate for the President of your club to wind up in prison."

Not bothering to say another word I hang up the phone, and then repeatedly punch my fist into my desk.

Thankfully, it's solid wood. Otherwise it would never withstand my temper.

A few minutes later, I send out a text to all the men to call an emergency church meeting. I want everyone to go to all our locations and get an accounting of all the women to be sure they are all still okay.

My mind flashes with thoughts of Katrina so I text Cross who messages right back that she is currently at work and all is good.

I sigh in relief. Knowing that Cross will keep an eye on her, I head to the meeting room to wait for all my guys.

This is so fucked up. I'm sure all our girls are fine. Surely if any had gone missing, someone would have alerted me by now.

Several hours later I have all the brothers spread out across the state to check on all the safe houses.

Animal, the one usually the loudest in the room no matter the circumstance, was the quietest during the meeting which doesn't bode well in my opinion.

I already don't like the stupid fuck and something tells me he's been up to no good.

Katrina

Several hours into my shift, Skeeter finally shows up. I was getting worried because I've become accustomed to him being there every night that I work.

The first few times that I noticed some of these women trying to get his attention bothered me more than I care to admit.

One particular night that was a woman that was really pushy in getting his attention. Going so far as to sit directly into his lap.

Watching his instant reaction by dumping her into the floor had me laughing so hard I had to hide in the kitchen until I could stop.

The cooks probably thought I was a little crazy. They're probably right since I feel as though Skeeter is mine in some way. I'm the one he's here for even though no one knows that.

I know it though and look forward to wrapping myself around him on the back of his bike each night. By the time we make it back to the house, my entire body feels as though it's on fire and my clit throbs for attention.

I go to sleep each night with the smell of myself on my fingers and thoughts of him in my head.

Looking up at the table he's sitting at with Cross, I notice that his eyes look even more serious tonight than usual. He normally looks more relaxed, even while staring at the door out of the corner of his eye.

Yes, I've noticed how watchful he is at all times. I notice everything about the man.

How his muscles in his shoulders tighten if someone walks up behind him. The movement is so slight you'd miss it if not watching closely. The way his eyes seem to follow me around the room.

The small dimple in the middle of his chin that is hidden just under his dark beard. Still, I've dreamed of kissing that spot more often the last few days.

Thoughts of him have had me thinking about sex. Mainly because I have no memory of sex but surely I've done it before.

I know one thing, if I would have had sex with Skeeter before, amnesia or not, I couldn't have forgotten a single moment of it.

"Want to tell me who or what you are thinking about?"

His voice directly behind me causes me to jump a little, not expecting him to be there.

"What do you mean?" I feel my face start to flush at having been caught, although he has no idea what I was thinking.

He reaches over, rubbing my jaw line with his thumb before lifting my chin higher to look directly into my eyes.

"What put such a secret grin on those lips?" He whispers as his thumb glides across my bottom lip.

A small gasp escapes my mouth and he grins slightly back at me when I bite my lip where he just touched it.

"You ready to go?" He finally asks without an answer to his other question.

Stepping back away from him, hoping it'll clear the fog his touch induced, I shake my head.

"Yeah, let me grab my bag." I say in a rush, walking to the back before I can take a huge breath.

His touch does something to me and I'm not sure how much longer I can stop from throwing myself at him like the rest of these sluts roaming around the bar.

An hour later, we pull up in front of the house but this time he gets off the bike, walking with me to the door.

His phone goes off and he stops at the steps to read the message. His eyes bunch in the middle, causing what I call worry lines above his eyes.

"I want you to come stay at the clubhouse for a little while." He says distractedly, typing furiously on his phone.

"I'm okay here at the house. My room is nice." I answer, not sure why he would say something about me staying elsewhere.

Looking back up from his phone, his eyes pierce my own.

"You'll have your own room at the clubhouse."

Looking at his serious face, I wonder if something is going on that he doesn't want to tell me.

"Why?" My one word question has his brows rising.

I already know from being around him that he's not the type that's used to someone questioning him. Instead of saying more, I decide to wait for his answer, raising my own eyebrows.

His lips kick up at the corners in a small smile.

"So it's a no then?" He says.

"So you're not going to answer then?" I quip back with my own smile that draws a chuckle from him.

"There's just some stuff going on. For now, I'll make sure there's someone here to just keep an eye out for all you girls. I do want you to be careful though. Don't leave with anyone not in the club. Can you at least do that for me?"

"I guess so but I have to work." I answer after giving it a thorough thought.

What he's asking isn't something huge. It's a small thing really and if he feels it's warranted, taking extra care is what I'll do.

"If I can't be here, I'll have one of the guys take you to work. I'll be there each night to make sure you get back home."

His words make my stomach flip flop. Mostly because I know when he gives his word, he keeps it. He'll be there every night for me.

"Alright." I can tell that my simple answer pleases him.

"I'll see you tomorrow." He almost whispers, moving closer to me.

My heart races as he leans in, kissing the side of my mouth. My eyes close at the contact wanting so much more. Would he give it to me if I turned slightly so that our lips touched fully?

He pulls away before I can make up my mind to do it. I watch his retreating back before turning to the door and going inside.

Skeeter

Getting to my room back at the clubhouse, I lock my door then strip completely nude before climbing between my silk sheets.

Sheets that I used to love so much are now becoming the best torture devices that I have ever been up against.

Thoughts of Katrina invade my mind all hours of the day but at night, they are worse. I imagine her on her knees, looking up at me as her soft lips open for the head of my cock to slip in.

Her mouth would be like slipping into heaven. Hot, soft and slick. Her tongue, doing things to me that I've never experienced.

With my cock now once again hard as a brick, I wrap my hand around myself giving a hard squeeze.

My balls throb as I pump myself slowly at first then faster with each downward stroke.

In my mind I imagine pulling her off me and throwing her face down onto my bed and slamming as deep as I can go into her tight pussy from behind.

I'd wrap my hand around her throat just to hold her closer to me as I slam into her so hard her breasts bounce.

I stroke myself harder thinking about how good she'd feel on my cock. It's not until I imagine her coming hard and squeezing me from deep inside that I come with a vengeance in my own hand.

Reaching to the bedside table, I grab something to wipe myself off.

Lying back with my arm thrown over my eyes, I try to catch my breath.

If the real her is anything like my imagination, I'm likely to die if I ever get her into my bed.

Then again, that would be a hell of a way to go out.

Chapter 5
Katrina

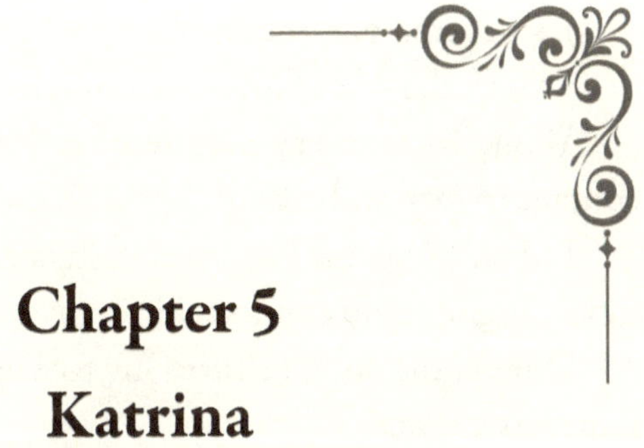

Skeeter has kept to his word. Over the past week, there's always been one of the guys from the club around the house.

Most usually staying outside on the porch. Only the one called Animal comes inside to flirt with the girls.

The times that he's here, I try to stay in my room so that I don't have to be around him.

I don't like the feeling I get when he's close by and I certainly don't like the way he looks at me.

Skeeter has always been the one to bring me home from work though which I've been grateful for.

He has no idea how much I love being on the back of his bike. I just don't think I could ride with anyone else.

Our Friday nights are always super wound up but tonight we were packed to capacity.

The guys at the door had to turn some away as there was no room left inside.

Pulling up in front of the house, I get off the bike and Skeeter of course follows.

It's become our routine lately where he walks me to the door, kisses the side of my mouth and leaves.

While I love every minute of it, I've still not gotten the courage to turn and take his lips with my own.

I often wonder if I was such a shy person before or if I was more outgoing and comfortable in my own skin.

Once at the door, he turns my face up to his, giving me the same kiss as usual.

"See you tomorrow?" I ask, looking back down at my toes.

"See you tomorrow." He answers with a grin.

Going inside the house, I close the door behind me and walk straight to my room.

A few beers got spilled on me tonight and I can't wait to get a shower.

Old beer starts to smell bad after a while.

Grabbing my clothes, head to the shower right across the hall, making sure to lock the door behind me.

A few minutes later, I'm relaxed with the hot water beating down on my back and the smell of my shampoo overtaking the beer smell.

Closing my eyes under the spray of the shower, my mind conjures up Skeeter's face with that sexy ass grin of his.

My nipples tighten and tingle as I think about his eyes looking at me. Unable to resist, my hands slide up my stomach to cup my breasts that now feel full and heavy.

As my fingertips slide across my nipples, it sends a shock wave all the way to my center.

My clit throbs wanting attention.

I imagine him in the shower with me. He's on his knees in front of me, his lips hovering over my clit. His tongue slipping out and licking my core.

My hand glides down and circles my clit, giving it attention as I imagine him doing it with his mouth.

I'm so close to coming, I squeeze my left nipple between my fingers.

The pleasure pain is so intense my head falls to the side against the wall.

My fingers strum faster along my clit but I need more.

Reaching down with my other hand, I slip two fingers inside myself.

The fullness as I pump my fingers in and out coupled with my clit getting so much attention, I fall over that precipice quickly.

I bite my bottom lip to hold in my moan of pleasure so that the other girls can't hear me.

I lean against the wall for several long minutes to catch my breath.

Once my eyes finally open, I wash myself on shaky legs once more before getting out of the now cold shower.

If I've ever experienced anything half that amazing, surely I would remember it.

Imagine how good the real thing could be.

Skeeter

Once Katrina is inside the house, I walk over to Tanker who has been here at the house most of the day to watch over the girls.

"Anything unusual?" I ask.

"Not a thing, Prez. I will tell you though that a few of the chicks here don't even remotely act like women who went through trauma." He answers from his propped up position on the side of the house.

"I've heard." I comment, knowing what he's talking about.

Several of the brothers have made mention of certain girls trying to get them to have sex with them while they are here and on duty.

While that isn't something that would be a huge issue, my guys know they are not to touch any of these women even if it's offered by them.

We know that several of them have backgrounds that are a bit shady. Prostitutes are easy to get a hold of and stuck into sex trafficking. Some even enjoy it.

Regardless, my men are loyal to the club and to me.

"Are you my relief?" He asks a few minutes later.

"Yeah. I think Animal is supposed to be here tomorrow."

"Huh." He comments and I look at him.

"There a problem?" I ask, raising my brow.

"Not really. I just don't trust him at all."

I turn my attention fully to him. Tanker isn't one to say much. He does his job without so much as a single complaint about anything or anyone usually.

"There a reason?" I ask.

He shrugs his shoulders. "Not really. I'm just tired. I'll see you tomorrow, Prez."

I watch as he walks to his bike, getting on it and a few minutes later roars down the road.

I turn back to the porch and sit on the swing. The porch light is off, not that it matters. I love our hot summer nights. The full moon gives off more than enough to see everything.

I'm there for about an hour when I hear the door being opened.

Watching the entrance, I see Katrina's head pop out as she tries to see in the dark.

"What are you doing out here?" My words make her jump and I watch her hand come up to hold her throat.

"You scared the crap out of me! I thought Tanker was out here and was going to ask him if he wanted some hot chocolate."

His words make me chuckle thinking about a big ass Tanker sitting down for a cup of hot cocoa.

"He just left to get some sleep."

"So you're our protector tonight?" She walks fully out onto the porch, both hands holding a mug.

I can tell she just got out of the shower as her hair is wet. The smell of something fruity lingers in the air. The same fruity smell that I associate with her. My cock jumps behind my zipper.

"Just me for tonight."

"You want the hot chocolate then?" She holds out a mug to me.

Taking the cup from her, I scoot over on the swing making room for her. Sitting down next to me, her smell surrounds me and I move slightly trying to alleviate the tightness I now have in my jeans.

"So beautiful." She breathes out, looking up at the moon. But I'm looking at her only.

"Yes. Very beautiful." I whisper and she turns back to me.

I watch as she registers that I was meaning her. Her face is flushing red and I can't stop my hand from reaching up to touch her cheek.

"You give all my men hot chocolate?" I ask, bringing the mug to my lips.

"Not all of them." She quips, turning back to her own mug.

"So only certain ones. Should I be jealous?" I tease.

"Are you?" She looks back over at me.

"Am I what?" I smile.

"Jealous."

"That depends." I move a little closer to her.

"On what?" Her breath hitches up, her eyes directly on my lips.

I'm about to kiss the hell out of this woman if she doesn't stop staring at me like that.

"It depends on whether or not you look at them the way you look at me." I watch as once again her face flushes and her eyes move to her feet.

I reach over, pulling her face back up so that I can see her eyes.

"No." She barely says above a whisper and I freeze, not knowing what she's saying no to.

"No, what?" I ask.

"No, I don't look at them the same." Her answer pulls a grin from me and I gently let go of her face,

We sit in comfortable silence finishing off our hot cocoa, gently pushing the swing in the moonlight.

"You're off tomorrow." I say suddenly, having an idea.

"Yes, I am. Why?" She asks, looking back at me.

"Will you have dinner with me?"

I don't know what I'm doing. I've never before asked a woman to dinner. Hell, I've never even had to ask for sex from one.

She looks shocked by my invitation and I begin to almost fidget. No woman has ever gotten to me in this way.

"You don't have to." I shake my head nervously.

"I would love to actually." She answers and I turn back to look at her smiling face.

She stands up, taking the mug from my hand.

I watch her walk back to the front door and turn back to me.

"I'll pick you up around four."

She smiles back once again. "Goodnight, Skeeter."

"Goodnight, Kat." The nickname that just came out makes her giggle as she walks inside, shutting the door behind her.

I'm left on the porch swing with the biggest hard on I've ever had, but I certainly can't wait for tomorrow night.

Katrina

Back in my room, I can't stop smiling about Skeeter asking me out on a date.

It is a date, right? Of course it is. You don't ask a woman to dinner unless it's a date.

Climbing between my sheets, my stomach is fluttering with nerves at the thought of going out with him.

Finding him on the porch instead of Tanker earlier surprised me. Especially since I knew what I had been doing in the shower before I got dressed and fixed the hot cocoa.

Sitting next to him on the swing, I wondered if he could somehow tell what I had been doing while thinking about him.

When he got close enough to kiss me though, I wanted him even more.

I've imagined a hundred times what his lips against mine would feel like.

I seriously can't wait for tomorrow night.

Surely he'll finally kiss me and it'll be everything that I've imagined it to be?

Just what the hell am I going to wear?

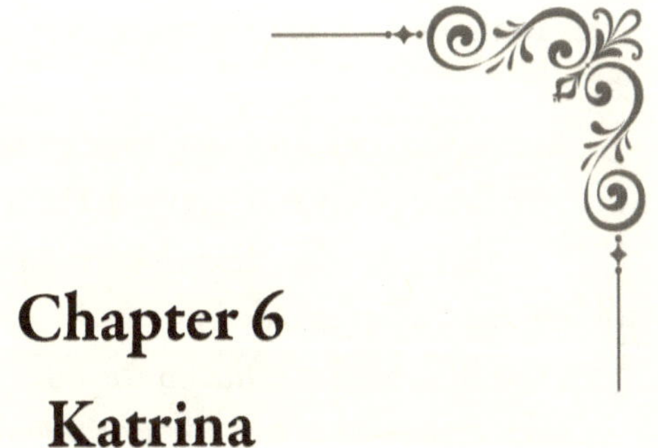

Chapter 6
Katrina

I'm ready to go by three forty five in the afternoon.

While I wasn't exactly sure what to wear, I went with a pair of jeans and a tank top in hopes that he would pick me up on his bike.

Walking into the kitchen for a glass of water, I don't notice anyone in the room until they start talking.

"Where are you off to?" Looking over to who's speaking, I see Krissy sitting on Animal's lap in a chair at the table.

"To dinner." I turn away from the two.

"With who?" Animal asks quickly.

While I don't want to answer him, I do anyway. He's one of Skeeter's men so I should be nice.

"Skeeter is coming to get me. He should be here soon." I answer but turn quickly to Skeeter's voice at the door.

"He's already here."

At Skeeter's voice the two at the table jump up as though someone splashed hot water on them.

"Aren't you supposed to be outside?" Skeeter growls at Animal.

Animal doesn't say anything, just moves to the door to leave.

Skeeter watches him leave, then turns back to me with a smile. I fidget not knowing if what I'm wearing is okay or not.

"I'm glad you wore jeans since I'm on my bike." He says, still looking me up and down.

"I was hoping you came on the bike." I smile widely.

"Like riding do you?" He grins, grabbing my hand as we walk to the front door.

As we make it to the porch he stops briefly looking over to where Animal is sitting.

"Cross will be here to relieve you from your post. I expect to see you in my office at the clubhouse at noon tomorrow."

Not waiting for Animal to reply, he turns away, pulling me along by the hand towards his big beautiful bike.

An hour later, we pull up to one of the nicest steak houses I've ever seen.

The place must be packed since the parking lot appears so full and I wonder if we have a reservation or if we'll have to wait for a table.

As we walk into the entrance, the hostess smiles at the two of us and immediately shows us to a table.

Taking a seat across from him, I look around the establishment and notice that they also have a live band as well as a dance floor on the other side of the restaurant.

"This is really nice. How'd you pull this off so quickly?" I look back at him.

Shrugging he says, "The owner owed me a favor."

The waitress walks up at that moment ready to take our orders. I can't stop smiling as Skeeter never once looks at the waitress, keeping his eyes directly on me.

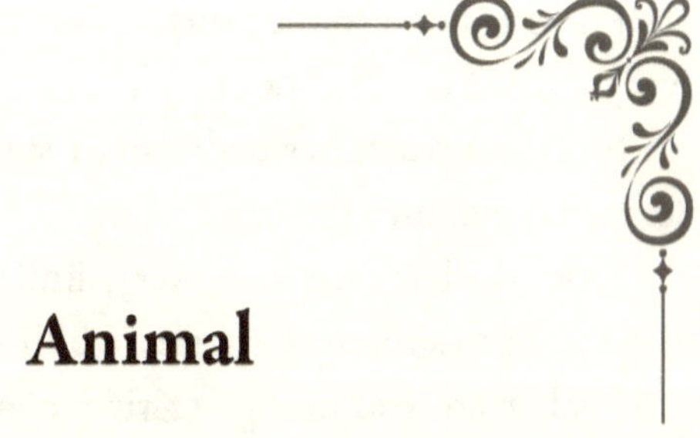

Animal

Watching the two of them leave, I want more than anything to rip Skeeter's eyes out of his head.

Who the fuck does he think he is anyway? He's clearly not keeping the same rules he's trying to force down our throats about these bitches.

Looking over at the door, Krissy smiles back at me. This is all her fucking fault.

If she hadn't caught me peeping at Katrina in the bath, I wouldn't have had to distract her from what she caught me doing.

I'm not due to deliver the other girl for another couple of days. Thinking about what I could do with her until then, my cock jerks in my jeans.

They ordered me not to touch them myself as they want them without bruising for the buyers they've found for them.

I'm only supposed to take the ones they indicate so that it's less noticeable by anyone.

Skeeter has yet to notice the ones that are missing from the safe houses up in Slidell.

"Skeeter's gone. You want to come to my room?" Krissy grins, letting the shoulder strap of her tank slip down, revealing the top of one tit.

Pushing her into the house, I look around making sure that everyone else is still gone as well.

Once we reach her bedroom, I spin her around and push her face down into the bed.

From the back she looks very similar to Katrina. One bitch that I want to sink my cock into a billion times.

"What are you doing?" Krissy complains, but I push her face down again.

"You want this; you'll take it exactly how I give it to you." I growl into her ear.

Pushing my jeans down to my thighs, my cock springs out, dripping from the end.

Pushing her shirt up because she is already bare underneath, I slam into her pussy in one fast thrust.

Her scream is muffled by the mattress, my hand still on the back of her head. I close my eyes, thinking of Katrina's face as I slide out and do it again.

The bitch under me, loving every thing that I'm doing to her. She spreads her legs wider so that I go deeper inside.

Imagining Katrina on my cock, I go faster, my balls getting even more firm, ready to explode.

Removing my hand from her head, I grab her hips to slam her back onto me even harder.

She moans, her pussy even wetter than before as our bodies slap together.

"I'm coming!" She moans. Her pussy tightening inside. I slam in once more and explode inside of her.

I stay where I am, as my cock throbs through the pleasure but its short lived once she turns her head to look at me.

She's a poor substitute for the real thing. It's time I put my plan into motion.

Skeeter

Talking with Katrina over dinner, I realize that I've not been this relaxed in years. At least not with a woman whom I truly enjoy talking to.

She asked a lot of questions about my past which I answered easily.

I grew up with my grandparents who passed away right after I graduated high-school. Not knowing what else to do with my life, I signed up for the marines.

I thought very seriously about making a full career out of it but after ten years of seeing some of the worst shit you could ever see, I decided to come back home to New Orleans.

After a year of being home, several of the guys I met in the service came for a visit. One of which was Grease who happened to be in the Night Howler's MC up in North Mississippi.

Over a lot of drinks out at my grandparents' house in the Bayou, which I still own, we came up with the idea of creating our own branch of the Night Howler's right here in the city.

That's exactly how we came to be and have grown quite a bit since we started nearly three years ago.

A club family that takes care of each other. We help all our guys keep a job, make sure they have a roof over their head and that they never wind up on the street like so many other Vets across this country.

"And saving women?" Katrina asks.

"That part is kind of new." I shrug, standing up from the table. "Come dance with me." I hold my hand out to her waiting.

I can't wait to hold this woman close to me. It's all I've thought about recently.

She places her hand in mine and I lead the way across to the middle of the dance floor. Turning to her, I slowly reach around her middle and pull her in.

The second I feel her body heat against me, my own heart beats fast against my chest.

It only takes her a minute to put her arms around my neck and lay her head on my shoulder. The smell of her shampoo hits my nose and I take a deep breath.

Moving my mouth to the shell of her ear, I whisper, "Is this okay?" as my hands slide down to rest just above her ass.

Instead of answering, she just shakes her head yes. I feel her breathing more heavily than before.

Wanting to test the waters a bit further, I make sure my lips are touching her ear this time when I speak.

"I've thought of this all day."

I feel her gasp but her body seems to move further into my own. I continue holding her as we dance slowly. Our bodies move together perfectly.

The song finally coming to an end, I let her go just enough to bring her face to my own.

Watching for any sign that she doesn't want this, I move in, placing my lips on hers. Her mouth opens slightly at my touch so I go in for a deeper kiss.

She kisses me back automatically but what makes me smile is when her hands fist my shirt as she tries to pull me closer.

Katrina

Oh my god, what a kiss. My lips tingle with sensation as we walk hand in hand towards the exit.

Getting to the bike, he helps me with my helmet and I can barely look up at him without feeling my face getting hot.

"I want to show you something before I take you home. Is that okay?" He asks, standing next to the bike.

I'm almost giddy that the night isn't going to end as soon as we get on the bike and roar down the road.

It's not long that I realize we are headed out of the city and further into the Bayou.

When we pull up to a small cabin in the middle of nowhere, my heart races knowing he's brought me to his grandparents house. His house.

Helping me from the bike, we leave my helmet on the seat and walk up onto the porch. Instead of going inside though, we follow the porch around to the back which is overlooking the Bayou.

The moon shining across the water is beautiful. The only sounds are of the animals and water.

"This is beautiful." I sigh.

"I thought you might like it. Come sit down, I'll go get you a blanket. You have goosebumps."

Now that he mentions it, the night air is a little cooler blowing off the water. Sitting down on the cushioned bench, I wait for him to go inside and get a blanket.

He comes back a few minutes later with two cups of hot chocolate as well as the blanket.

"My favorite! Thank you!" I giggle, taking the mug he offers me.

"I figured it was when I asked the guys if they've all had your hot cocoa." I laugh as he almost sounds jealous.

Sitting back with me in the seat, he pulls the blanket over the both of us, wrapping one arm around my shoulders.

As we just sit in silence, listening to the sounds around us, I get more comfortable by laying my head over on him. His hand begins rubbing circles on my upper arm.

I shiver from the touch and he looks down into my eyes.

"Still cold?" He asks huskily.

"Maybe a little." I answer.

Taking both our mugs and setting them on the table next to us, he reaches over and pulls me onto his lap, wrapping me tightly to him.

"Better?"

All I can do is shake my head as we stare into each other's eyes.

"Katrina, if you don't stop looking at me that way, I'm not sure I can stop myself from touching you." He growls.

My eyes widen at his words but I still don't look away from him.

"Kat!" He growls once more but I shake my head at him.

"I want you to touch me." I finally whisper.

As he looks into my eyes, he seems to almost snarl like a wolf then slams his mouth onto mine.

This kiss is not sweet like the one at the restaurant. Oh no. This kiss is brutal. Almost a claim and my body is on fire with wanting.

Without letting go of my mouth, his hands glide under my shirt, one up my back and the other straight to my breasts.

As his hand fondles me through my bra, the one at my back seems to snap the clasps releasing my breasts in the front.

Pulling my shirt up in the front, exposing me to his eyes, his mouth latches on and I throw my head back as I groan at the contact.

I'm almost coming from that one little thing already and don't notice when my shirt is pulled over my head.

Spinning me around, he lays me down on the bench as his mouth kisses down my stomach. I look down into his eyes as he gets to the button of my jeans.

With his eyes looking right at me, he unbuttons them and pulls them to my thighs. My pink lace panties are the only thing between my core and his mouth.

"I need to know if you taste as good as you smell." He whispers, his nose coming into contact with my clit under the panties.

I'm breathing so hard and my heart is racing so fast, I feel almost faint.

His fingers slowly pull my panties down just far enough to expose my center. I'm mesmerized as he slowly leans even closer and licks me straight up between my lips.

My face flushes as I watch him do it again.

"Take your hands and grab above your head." I do as he asks.

He reaches with both hands and snaps the fabric of my panties on both sides. With me watching he sticks them into his pocket.

Reaching up with his hands, he plays with my nipples, pulling them into stiff peaks. My clit is throbbing for attention and I move slightly trying to get some relief.

"I've got you baby. Just hold still." He whispers.

Then all I feel is the heat of his mouth as he dives his tongue into me several times before moving to my clit.

His tongue is like a machine gun as it flicks my clit rapidly for several long minutes at the same time his mouth is sucking me in.

"Oh god!" I throw my head back as I feel myself climbing higher towards my own release.

Not realizing my eyes are squeezed shut, they pop back open quickly when I feel the fingers of one of his hands at my entrance. Two fingers slowly make their way into me.

He moves them around quickly in and out before a third finger has me feeling completely full.

It's just like that with his mouth on my clit and his fingers inside of me that I scream out my release across the Bayou.

Skeeter

I lick every drop of her as she comes down from her orgasm. Her taste in my mouth has my cock throbbing for release.

As she finally looks at me, I stand up and scoop her into my arms, walking us both into the cabin.

Getting to my bed, I lay her down gently onto my sheets as I strip off my own clothes.

Her breathing once again hitching up and I'm enthralled by the rise and fall of her breasts.

Slowly getting on the bed next to her, I just watch for a sign from her.

If she doesn't want to do anything else, I'll stop now. I may have to go take a long cold ass shower though.

She finally reaches up, pulling my face down to hers.

I take her lips willingly and she pulls her body against my own.

Knowing that she's already wet from what I did to her on the porch, I reach for my pants and find a condom.

Ripping it open, I put it on quickly without breaking our kiss.

Moving over the top of her, her body fits mine perfectly.

Rubbing my length along her wetness first, I line myself up with her center and as slowly as I can, push into her tight heat until I'm completely inside.

Staying still so she gets used to me there, one of my hands falls to her nipple, pinching it just enough to get her attention.

Her nipples are almost like the control buttons for her pussy.

Every pinch of her nipple makes her pussy tighten around my cock and I growl from the feeling.

I pull back slowly until I'm just barely inside of her and slam back in.

"Ugh." She cries out in pleasure so I do it again, building up a rhythm that will hopefully have us both going over that edge together.

I'm so close already but I strain to hold back, waiting for her.

Grabbing her head with my hands and my mouth still on hers, I growl, "Come Kat! Come now!"

Slamming back into her one more time, she screams out as I feel her pussy squeezing me from within and I explode into the condom so hard I'm afraid it might have broken.

I kiss her gently as we both try to catch our breaths. By the time I finally pull completely out of her, she looks half asleep.

Tossing the condom into the trash can, I curl around her, pulling her as close as I can and we both fall asleep.

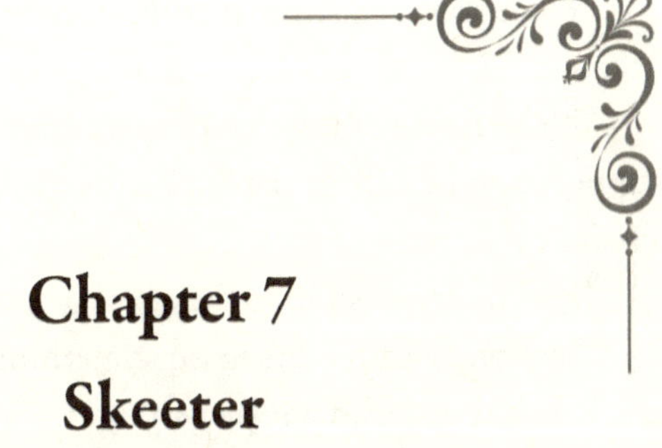

Chapter 7
Skeeter

Walking into the clubhouse after dropping Katrina off at the house this morning, I look around to see if Animal has gotten here yet.

If he thinks he's getting away with what happened yesterday when I picked up Katrina, he's badly mistaken.

All the men know not to mess with the girls in any way even if they are the ones trying to get your attention.

Our club has to keep a good reputation where these girls are concerned. Most of them are traumatized by the situations that we save them from.

The girls or women rather, need to be able to trust us to keep them safe. Even from ourselves.

"What's up, Prez?" Looking to my left I see Buzz walking towards me with a huge grin.

"From the look of your face, I'd say Markayla finally moved in with you." I smile back at my friend that deserves some happiness in his life.

"She damn sure did. Took her long enough!" He grouches and I just chuckle at him.

"Have you seen Animal around anywhere this morning?" I ask.

"Nah. And I meant to tell you that a contact of mine is supposed to be calling me back on what you asked me about." He raises his brows.

"Let me know soon as they get back to you."

"You really think he's in on something?" He asks.

"Yeah, I do. And another thing. I caught him in the house with the girls yesterday. Him and Krissy all over him."

"I told you that Krissy was going to be an issue. She still isn't working anywhere either."

I look over to him quickly, having not known that last bit of information.

"Thought she went to work at the grocery store?"

He shrugs his shoulders, "I was told she got fired for flirting with customers."

"We may have to meet with her and tell her like it is. Our houses are for temporary situations. Just until they get back on their feet." I sigh.

"I'll go by and see if I can get her to understand."

I nod as he heads towards the door but I stop him before he leaves.

"Might want to take some back up. I'd hate for Markayla to kill your ass for smelling like another woman." I tell him.

"Who do you think I'm going to take with me?" He laughs back, closing the door behind him.

After Buzz leaves, I head into my office to wait for Animal. I also message Grim and make sure he's able to take Katrina to work.

I'll be there to pick her up at closing and hopefully, she'll go back home with me again tonight.

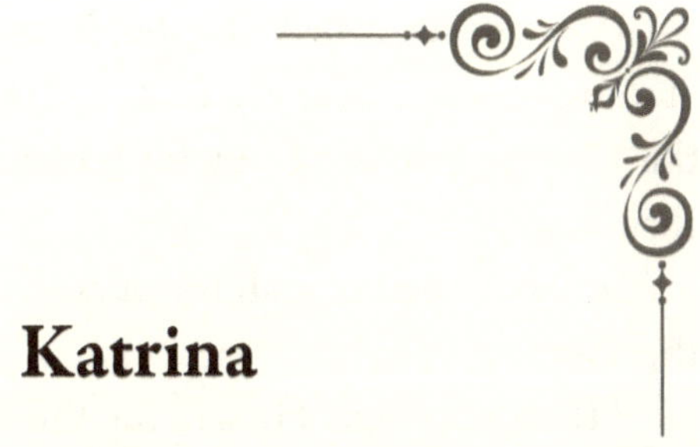

Katrina

This shift seems as though it's taking forever to end but I know it's because I keep looking at the clock every few minutes.

Skeeter won't be here for another hour at least as he doesn't usually get here to wait for me until a few hours before closing.

Making several more rounds of drinks for the guys in the corner, I realize that my trash can behind the bar is starting to get full.

Waving over one of the other girls to continue taking orders at the bar, I grab the bag and head out the back to take it out.

As I open the back door, I remember to move the block so that the door doesn't shut all the way and lock me outside.

Dropping the bag in the dumpster, I realize someone else is in the alley with me. My heart races at first, not knowing who it is until he speaks.

"It's just me." Animal steps into the light so that I can see him.

While it calms me to know who it is, I still don't like this guy for some reason.

"Oh, hey Animal. Is something wrong?" I ask.

"Skeeter just called." He holds up his phone in his hand. "I'm supposed to take you somewhere safe." He looks around the alley as if looking out for someone to jump out of the shadows.

"Okay. I need to grab my purse first." I start back towards the door.

"There's no time. He said the threat is likely inside the bar already. We gotta go. Now!" The urgency in his voice propels me forward.

He grabs hold of my arm, walking me faster down the alley. At the other end, in the darkness is a car that I've never seen before and my legs lock up on me.

I feel something hard poke me in my side. Looking down, I see a gun held by Animal.

"Get in the fucking car!" He growls.

I start to scream but the world goes black around me as pain shoots through my head.

Skeeter

"Heard about you ripping Animal a new one." Grim chuckles from the seat across from me.

"He finally show up this morning?" Buzz asks, looking over.

"Yeah. Three fucking hours later than the time I told him to be here." I growl into the beer in my hands.

Today was a long day going through all the paperwork on the various businesses that the club now owns across the state.

"How's the new strip club coming along? I heard that some of the flooring was on backorder." Pops asks, pulling up a chair with his wife, Renee right behind him.

"I still can't believe you boys are opening yet another strip club." She shakes her head.

"The flooring should still be here in plenty of time." I answer Pops. Looking over at his sweet wife, I can't stop the smile I give to her. She's like the mother that so many in the club need.

"Sex sells sweetheart. Even if it's not something you can actually touch." Pops pats her hand but she huffs at his statement.

Pops is right though. Sex or the illusion of sex sells easily. Even if the economy is hell, the strip clubs will bring in revenue.

Someone's phone rings and I automatically reach into my pocket only to realize that I left my phone in my office.

"Fuck!" Buzz blurts out, whipping his head from his phone over to me. "We'll be right there!" He screams into the phone before hanging up.

The rest of us have stood up, ready to leap at whatever the issue is.

"We gotta go. Katrina is missing." He says.

My heart pounds, wondering what has happened. She was supposed to be at work. I know she was at work because I checked in with Cross just an hour ago.

Not stopping to get any details right this moment, my boys and I run out to our bikes. Passing a couple of the prospects, I send them to the house where she's been living since getting out of the hospital. There's still a chance she just went home.

With hope in my heart that she did just that, I roar down the road to the bar.

Fuck! Just let her be alright!

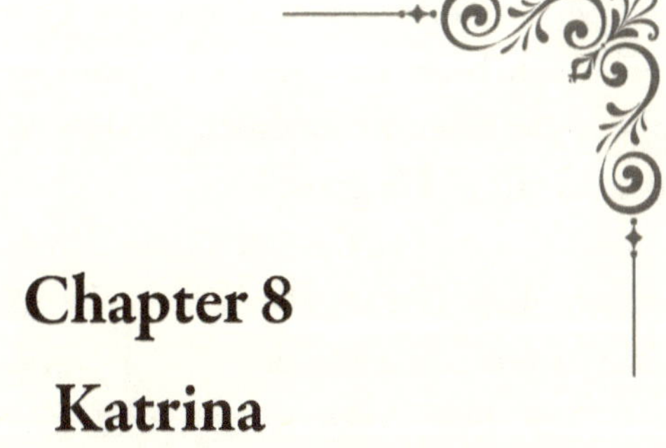

Chapter 8
Katrina

As my eyes open the first thing I notice is the throbbing in my head. Trying to move my hand up, I realize that I'm tied down.

With one eye open, I take a look around. This asshole has me tied to the bed, spread out like some sacrifice to the Gods or something.

Pulling slightly on my bindings, the zip ties he used cut into my skin and I know there's no way for me to break it.

Closing my eyes, my head swims with what might be memories of being tied down before. I see a room that's dark but the memory is gone before I can completely grasp it.

My heart races and I begin to sweat. I must be close to a panic attack. I close my mouth and breathe slowly through my nose which seems to help a little.

I'm still trying to figure out a way to break the ties holding me when I hear footsteps close to the door. I slam my eyes closed just as the door swings open hoping he'll think I'm still asleep.

"I brought you something to eat my sweet kitten." He says softly, closer to the bed this time.

My eyes remain closed until I feel him touching my arm.

"Such beautiful eyes. That was the first thing I noticed about you when we first met. Too bad you don't remember our first meeting." He grins.

"You mean at the safe house." I finally speak, wondering why he'd think I wouldn't remember the first few days after Skeeter moved me there.

"Not there. At the courthouse. You were magnificent that day." He chuckles, untying just one of my hands and handing me a cup that smells like soup.

Taking the offering from his hand, I hope that he will continue talking. I don't remember anything he's talking about. Why would I be at a courthouse?

"How was I magnificent?" I sip the soup hoping like hell it's not drugged.

"The whole room was enthralled by the story. You really don't remember?" His brows scrunch together as he looks at me hard, then his face changes drastically.

"I should have taken you first all those years ago instead of that bitch of a sister of yours."

Another face flashes in my head. One very similar to my own, smiling back at me.

My eyes fill with tears.

"Julie?" The name pops out of my mouth automatically.

Animal smiles evilly. "Sweet little Julie. She was such a good girl. Always did what she was told."

Other memories begin to assail me. Julie with a man who I can't remember. How he used her in so many ways, both sexually and physically.

The soup I was drinking now threatened to come back up my throat as I remember the night she died.

I had been trying to reach her for days but she never would call me back so I went over to the house where they were staying.

No one came to the door so I went around looking into the windows. The last window on the back side of the house is where I watched the life drain from my own sister.

The man she had been with for so long was standing at the door, while another man had her tied to the bed and was fucking her from behind while choking her with a cord.

She began thrashing around, indicating that she couldn't breathe. I must have knocked over a trash can because all eyes moved to the window I had been peeping through.

I ran as fast as I could to a store down the street and called nine one one. By the time the cops got there, my sister was dead and the men responsible were gone.

They concluded that it was all part of a huge human trafficking ring and made me go into witness protection.

Grabbing the cup from my hand making me jump from the memories, he slams it down on the table next to the bed and grabs my hand, tying it to the bedpost once more.

At the door, he turns back around looking right at me.

"Should really remember when you put a man's brother away for life." He growls, slamming the door behind him.

All of this apparently has something to do with the things I can't remember from before. As for what all of that is, I still have no clue.

Tears stream down my face as I remember my sweet sister. The sister I couldn't save.

I cry for what seems like hours before I fall asleep.

I wake myself up, screaming into the darkness of the bedroom.

The door crashes open at the same time that Animal turns on the light.

"Stop that fucking screaming before I gag your ass!" He yells.

My eyes are blurry from tears but I watch his face as he looks down at my breasts.

Glancing down, I realize that my tank top has gotten twisted in my sleep, exposing one breast that is still covered by my bra.

Probably from all the thrashing I was doing from the bad dreams that all the memories forced onto me.

My eyes widen as his hand reaches out, grabbing the side of my tank and pulling it back over in a way that allows his hand to rub across my breast.

He growls low in his throat, reaching to adjust himself. I shiver in revulsion but he takes it another way.

"You like that don't you? What you do to me? We had some good times before, didn't we?" He grabs my breast in his hand, squeezing hard enough that I gasp in pain.

"Soon beautiful. Soon you will look at me the same way you look at that stupid fuck Skeeter. Then I'll take you for the ride of your life."

"I will never look at you that way." I find the courage to say.

He chuckles, grabbing my face and leaning in close.

"You fucking will or you'll pay like you did before. I paid good money to have your cunt and I will have it!"

He lets go of my face and I'm certain there will be bruises where his fingers were at but I don't drop my gaze from his.

He turns back to the door but before he closes it behind him, I say one last thing.

"He's coming for me you know and he's going to fucking kill you."

He looks back at me with a hard expression before grinning again.

"Not if I kill him first."

He slams the door once again and I finally take a gulp of air into my lungs.

"Please find me before its too late." I whisper into the silence of the room.

Skeeter

The sun is just coming up when I pull up at my grandparents' old house.

Climbing off my bike, I grab the whiskey bottle I brought with me from my saddle bags.

Stepping up onto the porch, my eyes land on the bench seat where Katrina and I were sitting together a little more than twenty four hours ago.

Turning around, I plop down onto the top step and stare out across the bayou.

"Fuck!" I scream out, taking the top off the bottle and taking large gulps.

As soon as we had gotten to the bar last night, we canvassed the area.

Checking the surveillance cameras at the bar picked up nothing as someone had cut the feed from the back alley.

The last the camera's saw of her was when she walked through the kitchen toting garbage out the back door.

That's where they took her from and they left no traces of her at all.

Her purse which was left at the bar is now currently in my saddle bags, not that it would help us at all.

Katrina is basically a ghost. There was no trace as to who she really is or where she came from.

I prop up on the step I'm sitting on and drink in complete silence.

When my phone rings, I'm tempted to ignore it but there's still a chance that someone has found her.

Picking it up, I don't recognize the number but I answer anyway.

"Yeah." I growl over the line.

"I heard that you are missing someone."

"Who the fuck are you?" I say through clenched teeth, not recognizing the voice.

"Oh, I'm sorry that we've not been properly introduced. I'm Special Agent Newman, Mr. Landry."

"Agent Fox has never mentioned you."

"Of course he hasn't. That little piss ant has been trying to work his way up the ladder and make a name for himself." He huffs over the line.

"So what do you want? Why are you calling me?" I pick up my whiskey and toss it back, realizing that it's almost empty.

If I ever stand up, I'll probably fall flat on my face.

"We need you to get her back."

"Who?" I ask, trying to make sure we are on the same page.

"Katrina, Mr. Landry. Keep up."

"Watch your tone mother fucker." I growl but all he does is chuckle. "Why does the Bureau all of a sudden care about Katrina?"

"We've always cared. Well, at least I have. She's the only witness still alive that has ever seen the face of the man that controls the largest trafficking ring in the South."

Sitting up quickly, I nearly fall from the porch.

"What the fuck? Why isn't she in protective custody?" I demand.

"She was but somehow they found out her location and took her. When she was found in that warehouse with so many others, we were glad she was found. We would have moved her to another location but realized she had lost her memories."

"So basically since she couldn't remember anything she was useless to you?" I say through gritted teeth.

"Look, Mr. Landry..."

"It's Skeeter you mother fucker. I'll get her back but you son of a bitches won't be touching her! You got that? Unless you have suggestions as to where she might be, don't fucking call me again!" Hanging up the phone, I slam it down on the porch, cracking the screen.

Trying to stand up, the world spins around me so I sit back down. Picking up my phone again, I dial Buzz's number.

That mother fucker better still be awake. I need help getting off this fucking porch and I seriously need some damn coffee!

Katrina

I've been awake since the sun came up and started shining through the window.

Animal hasn't been back in here since he stormed out late last night.

I was hoping that I wouldn't have to draw attention to myself but I've seriously got to go to the bathroom which means I'm going to have to call him in here if he doesn't show up soon.

A lot more of my memories have flooded back since last night as well. My real name really is Katrina and I'm from Ohio.

I originally came down here to look for my sister. She had moved here after finding some guy she was convinced was the love of her life.

Towards the end, her phone calls got more sporadic and I always felt like she was in over her head.

In our last phone conversation, she had let it slip about where they were staying.

Her words were all slurred at the time and when I asked her about it, she told me that this was her life to live.

I only got to talk to her once in person when I arrived in New Orleans before she was killed.

Looking back on that day, I know she was scared for me instead of for herself as she told me to leave and never come back.

I did come back though. That very same night. The night that I watched her die, unable to help her at all.

They put me in witness protection after everything. A lot of good that did.

Hearing footsteps getting closer, I brace myself for Animal to come through the door. Slamming it open, he just stands there staring.

"I need to pee." I finally say.

Without saying a word, he walks just outside the door and brings back a rope. My eyes widen, not sure of his intent.

He unties my arms first, quickly tying them together in the front before he moves to my legs, wrapping the rope around both before securing it altogether so that I can only raise my arms if my legs raise as well.

Jerking me from the bed he pushes me into the hall, stopping at the first door we come to.

He pushes me in before turning on the light and I realize there's no window in here.

"Go ahead." He smirks, standing with his arms crossed.

I know he doesn't plan to look away and I hope that my tank will come down far enough to hide me at least a little bit while my pants are down.

This is more humiliating than most anything else I've ever suffered. He's done this to me before though.

While I was in that warehouse I watched helplessly as he hurt other women in front of me.

He'd always tell me just before, that I could spare them the pain if I'd just give in to him willingly.

I still have no idea why it was so important to him to have my blessing to take my body when he took other women forcibly.

He spent months trying to break me until one night he was the one that snapped.

That was the beating that caused so much damage. The same night that the club saved me. The night Skeeter saved me.

I look up at him with narrowed eyes the whole time that I pee.

This crazy bastard didn't break me before and he won't break me now.

Chapter 9

Skeeter

I punch the bag in front of me hard enough to jar my teeth but I don't stop. Not even to wipe the sweat pouring from my face.

Katrina and several others from various safehouses are all now missing.

That can only mean one fucking thing. There's a rat in my club.

The truly fucked up part is, that I don't have a clue as to who it could be. Our club is built on trust and loyalty above all things.

The Feds don't want us working with them right now because of it. They know there's a rat too. Until I ferret the bastard out, we are all out of work.

What's even more fucked is that I have to find a way to tell my club brothers without letting it known to them that we have a traitor.

I've got to catch this stupid fuck but I can't do it alone. I only know of one brother that is without a doubt loyal to not only me but to this club.

Hopefully, with his help and his expertise on the computer, we can take a closer look at our brothers' extra curricular activities beyond our club doors.

Maybe then, we can get those girls back. My sweet Katrina back. We promised them safety. So far, we've failed miserably.

Punching the bag one last time, I head towards the showers. No one stops me on my way. They all know I'm in a mood.

My temper precedes me. Whoever this fucker is, he apparently doesn't know his Prez all that well.

It's time he was introduced to him.

Back in my office, I shoot off several quick texts calling all the guys in for a Church meeting.

I schedule it for late in the day so that all the guys that are all over the state get back in time for it. I then send out a private text to Buzz asking him to meet me at his place.

If there's one person that can find something useful on any of these fuckers, he's the one to do it.

He's been distracted lately with his own problems. His sister is slowly trying to get back to her life as best she can since she was taken and his woman, Markayla just recently moved in with him.

Grabbing my keys, I head out the door not saying a word to any of the brothers that are already here. For all I know, the traitor could be any one of them.

Twenty minutes later, I pull up to a gate that opens automatically when I get close to it.

This is my first time at his new place that is even farther outside of the city than the last one.

As I get closer to the building, Buzz is standing at the front door waiting for me.

"How's the head?" He grins widely.

"It's just fine you fucker! If I'd known you'd keep on about it, I'd have just slept on the porch!" I growl back.

Looking around at his new digs, I'm impressed by just the size of it.

"Do you think you could get even further out of the city?" I ask, turning off my bike.

"I needed to place longer range surveillance systems so that I could see the enemy coming a lot sooner than last time. This place was perfect." He chuckles as I shake my head.

"What is it that you need that couldn't wait until Church?" He holds the door open for me to walk inside.

You'd never believe that people actually live here judging from the outside of the place. Inside is one of the nicest houses you've ever seen.

"I need you to do an even deeper check on any of our guys that have come into the club in the past year. I didn't text you this just in case our phones have been compromised in some way."

He raises his brows. "Seriously?"

"Yeah. There are more girls missing from some of our other safehouses. While we recently changed the rules on how to become a club member, up until almost a year ago our only requirement was that you were former military."

"You really think one of our guys would be walking on the dark side?" His expression goes hard.

Shrugging my shoulders, I answer honestly. "It's happened before. Lots of ex-military have come home and done some super fucked up things. Hell, some did fucked up things during war. We've both seen it."

"Yeah." He shakes his head. "Give me your phone." He holds his hand out and I give it to him without question.

"It's good you cut it off before getting here. Let me hook it to the computer real fast and scan it."

I follow him to his computer room and see all the screens going at once. Some are tapped into cameras that are spread out all over the city.

A few minutes later he hands my phone back to me.

"I didn't find anything on it but I did up your firewall protection. It should be good for now."

"Thanks man. There's something else." His brows raise waiting for me to continue

"I was contacted by a Special Agent Newman. He says that Katrina was in witness protection before she was taken to that warehouse where we found her. I need you to find those files. Whatever it takes. I have a feeling it's all connected somehow."

"No problem. I'll see what I can find before heading to the club for Church. Whatever I find, I'll keep it to myself until we can speak freely."

With a quick nod, I see myself out and Buzz immediately turns to his computer. I hear the gate lock engage as soon as I'm through it on my bike.

Pulling out into the road, I head back to the club to wait for all my men.

Hopefully by tonight, I'll know who the traitor in my club is and as a club, we'll put the rabid dog to sleep.

Getting back to the club house, I scan the faces of the men that have already responded to the call I sent out earlier.

Several of them, I've known for years and would never suspect them of doing such a thing.

Although, what I told Buzz is true. Some of our men come home different.

Unable to assimilate back into "normal society", they turn to darker paths.

Most dying by suicide but sometimes, they take innocent lives before taking their own.

"Prez." Mick nods my way, offering me a beer that I decline with the shake of my head.

"Everyone here yet?" I ask.

"Not yet. There's still a few missing from the group." I shake my head in acknowledgement.

"You doing okay Prez?" Renee, Pops Ole lady asks, walking up to our little group.

Throwing my arm around her, I accept her hug willingly.

Instead of answering, I just smile down into her face. She must understand, as she just squeezes me tight for a few minutes before walking away.

"Tell Buzz to let me know when he gets here." I tell Mick before walking away.

Back in my office, I shut the door and then plop down on the couch on the other side of the room.

Closing my eyes for a few minutes, Katrina's face pops into my head.

I hope more than anything that she is okay. I've got to find her. I've been drawn to her since the first time I ever laid eyes on her.

I can't lose her now.

Katrina

It's been a while since Animal has come in here to check on me but I know he's still inside the house from all the noise coming from another room.

For the last hour I've been rubbing the ties on my wrists against the bed posts.

My arms are so sore and I feel blood trickling down but I'm determined to get loose before this crazy asshole does something truly sinister.

Hearing his steps getting closer to my door, I stop moving only to jump when he slams the door open.

Looking at my arms he comes further into the room with an evil grin.

"You'll slit your wrists if you keep pulling like that." His eyes rove over the rest of my body, spread out across the bed.

Reaching down to adjust himself, he looks back into my eyes.

"You should just give in to me. You'd love it." He whispers.

Revulsion rolls through me as I watch him looking at me and his pants getting tighter with an erection at my predicament.

"You are just as sick as your brother!" I growl through clenched teeth.

His hand, lightening fast, hits me across the face and I gasp at the pain that shoots through my head.

"You like it rough. I know you do. Your cunt of a sister did as well. Did I tell you that?" He grins as my eyes shoot to him. "Hmm, she was so hot for it too." He closes his eyes as if he's remembering her.

Tears leak from my own at the thoughts running through my head at what my sister must have endured. She was such a sweet girl.

"She thought she was too good for us too at first. The first time she choked on my cock, she learned to love it." He grins.

"Too bad she didn't bite the little fucker off." I grin back and get another hard slap but this time, I smile through it.

"We'll be leaving soon. Your bitch ass boy toy is making too many waves searching for you. He called in the whole club and when he sees that I'm not there, he'll be searching for me as well." He walks back towards the door.

"Where are we going?" I yell at him, my heart racing quickly.

He just looks back with a chuckle, and then slams the door shut.

With him finally out of the room and my face throbbing from his blows, I allow the tears in my eyes to finally fall.

I've been here before.

Taken against my will and held hostage by this sick fuck for several months before I was saved.

No one was actively looking for me then, though.

There's someone now.

There's Skeeter and hopefully he finds me before this bastard yet again gets me onto a cargo ship.

Skeeter

"Prez, I got all the files." Buzz barges into my office.

Sitting up in my chair, I wait for him to set up his computer on my desk.

"How bad is it?" I ask.

"This is some sick shit. I'll tell you that." Buzz says quickly, pulling up multiple pages on the screen.

"Here." He says, handing me the laptop.

As I read through the file, my stomach is in knots but I really feel sick when I come across the pictures taken at the scene of Julie's murder.

The only man ever caught was Brandon, Julie's supposed boyfriend that apparently lent her out to any man that was willing to pay.

He died within a month of being in the state pen. Stabbed to death by another inmate that accused him of having something to do with the disappearance of his own sister.

That inmate was already serving a death sentence and they say he laughed the whole time as blood sprayed all over the room.

The man that killed her is the only one still at large.

The bureau only knows him as Z because no one so far has ever been able to give a real name for the fucker.

"Jesus." I sigh, handing the laptop back to Buzz.

"Yeah. I can't imagine Katrina watching it happen and being unable to help." He gets lost in thoughts of his own sister whom we all thought was dead until recently.

"All the men here?" I finally ask, standing up.

"Don't know, I came straight in here to you."

"Let's go see if everyone showed up or not." Determined, I head for the door.

As I walk into the room, everyone quietens down and I take my time to look at all my brothers.

I notice one face that is missing from the crowd though and I feel a tick start in my jaw.

"Where's Animal?" I ask loudly.

"Anyone seen him lately?" Buzz asks.

"He's not been around here since you crawled his ass the other day, Prez." Tanker says.

"Buzz use that computer of yours and find a fucking connection!" I growl. My hands tighten into fists.

I knew deep down there was something off with that fucker.

"Oh fuck!" Buzz bursts out a few minutes later and we all crowd in behind him to look at the screen.

While the picture of the man Buzz has found is a little different, it's definitely Animal.

"Who the fuck is he?" I demand.

Turning to look at me with raised brows, Buzz answers. "His brother was the boyfriend that Katrina testified against in court."

Red hot rage pours through me and more than one brother backs up a little at the look on my face.

I try breathing through my nose to slow my heart beat. I can hear Buzz typing furiously on his keyboard.

"Got it! His family owns an old house not far outside the city." His computer beeps a few times and I look back at him. "Well, shit. That was easy." He laughs a little.

"What?" I demand.

"I tapped into his phone. Hold on, all the records from the last couple days are populating right now." He grins.

The man is truly in his element when it comes to computers and programs.

"I'm going to cross reference this list with what we got from the warehouse raid where we found Katrina."

He talks through his fingers flying across his computer.

"Got a hit. There's one number that he's called several times the last couple of days. One that I've been tracking for a while. It only gets turned on for a couple of minutes at a time each day. I've suspected it to be one of the transporters."

"You mean one of the ones that moves the girls from city to city?" Grim asks.

"Yeah." Buzz answers.

"So what do you want to do Prez?" Brick, who rarely says anything, asks as he cracks his knuckles.

"Pull up all the maps surrounding the house, Buzz. Make sure we get every single exit point covered. We're going in at dark. Just one thing." I say, looking around at all my men. "I want him alive."

They all shake their heads, knowing exactly what I plan to do.

We may have done some work with the bureau in our recent past. We are also ex-military but by God, we are also a club that doesn't always play by society's rules.

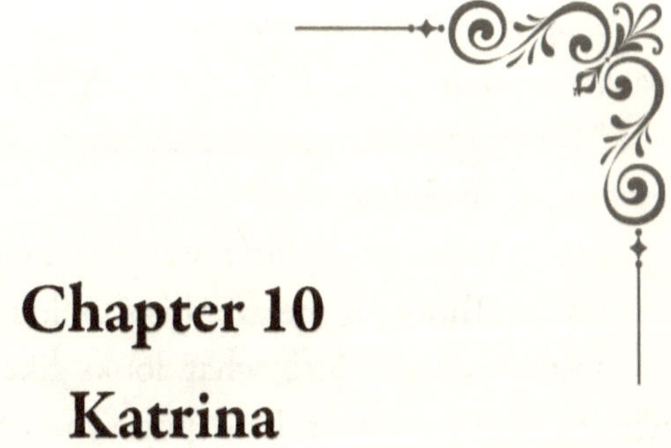

Chapter 10
Katrina

"You're fucking late!" Animal yells from the other room. I assume he's talking to whoever he had said would be here to give us a ride earlier.

Looking over at the window, I notice it's fully dark now. I guess he should be scared if Skeeter really does know that he's involved now.

Even though my wrist has been bleeding, I've not stopped rubbing the zip tie on the bedpost, hoping that it'll break.

When all of a sudden, my arm falls away from the post, I'm so surprised that it takes me nearly a minute to bring my hand closer to my face.

Reaching over to my other wrist, I try pulling with the strength of both my arms and the tie there gives too.

Rubbing my wrists for only a second, I sit up, reaching for my legs.

I'm concentrating so hard on what I'm doing that I don't hear Animal coming towards the room until the door bangs off the wall.

"What the fuck?" He yells, running over to the bed to grab me.

I fight as hard as I can, clawing his face. His fist swings back, clocking me right in my mouth and my head rolls.

"You stupid fucking cunt! As soon as we get on board, I'll make you pay for that!"

He jerks me up, tying my hands and feet in a way that I can't walk. Throwing me over his shoulder.

Just as we get into what looks like the living room, a window breaks with a loud pop. The entire room fills with smoke.

Skeeter

"Everyone in position?" I whisper over the coms. After every man checks in, I recheck my gun one last time.

"Remember. I want him alive, so no kill shots. Got it?" I growl.

Several yes sirs come at me.

"Grim. Go." As soon as I give the command, Grim shoots a smoke bomb into the living room window.

Not wasting any time, we rush to the house, taking positions at every door and window.

I hear a woman scream, although it didn't sound like Katrina to me.

"Buzz, have you infrared of the house?"

"Yep. There's more than just Animal and Katrina in there but I don't think they are friends of Animal."

"What you mean man?" Grim asks just as bullets hit the front door from inside the house.

"It's a large cluster, huddled together. Seems to be in the basement." He answers.

"Does anyone have line of sight of that fuck yet?" I growl.

"Yep." Tanker says over coms just before we hear a shot and Animal howls in pain.

"Please tell me you didn't fucking kill him!" I growl, standing up and heading towards the front door.

"Nope. But he's not going to be able to use his hands any time soon." Tanker laughs.

Getting to the door, I watch around the corner and see Tanker bent over Katrina who's lying on the floor.

Rushing over to her, I cut her bindings and turn her face to look into mine.

"You okay?"

I run my hands over her bruised face and try like hell to hold in my rage so that I don't scare her any more than she already appears to be.

"You came for me." She whispers through her tears and I hold her close to me.

Picking her up gently, I carry her out the door, still ignoring Animal who is screaming about his hands.

I'll deal with his ass shortly.

"Buzz, I need you to take Katrina back to my house." I say over coms.

"Be right there."

It'll only take him a minute to get here as he's just down the road in the surveillance van.

"I want to stay with you." She says weakly, holding me tighter.

Before I can say anything else, I hear Grim in my ear about there being women in the basement and that we'll need another van.

"I have some stuff to take care of and then I'll be there. Just go with Buzz right now please. He'll keep you safe."

Buzz pulls up, opening the side door.

"We're going to need another van." I tell him, setting Katrina inside the back.

"I heard." His mouth turns firm. "I'll send one of the prospects."

Nodding my head to him, I turn back to Katrina.

"I'll be there soon."

She just stares back at me, turning her head away.

I know that she needs more from me but I can't give it to her right now.

There are the other women to tend to as well as the asshole that took something that didn't belong to him.

Shutting the side door, I step back and Buzz rushes off back down the driveway.

Turning back to the house, my eyes narrowed to slits.

Before I start walking though, Grim grabs my shoulder.

"Let's take care of the girls inside first. Then you can have free reign."

Looking over at one of my closest friends, I just nod and head inside.

Looking over into the kitchen, I see that my men have Animal tied to a chair.

"Over here, Prez." Cross says from a door in the middle of the hallway.

Walking down the stairs, it's darker in the basement with only one light.

One of the guys hands me their flashlight and I walk over to another door to an even smaller room.

Looking inside, there's girls ranging in age but I don't recognize a single one of them as any of the girls still missing from our other safe houses.

"None of them are ours." I whisper.

"Nah. They are all scared. Figured I'd leave it to you to offer them a safe place to go or to be dropped off at the hospital."

Nodding my head, I step further into the room. The girls all squeeze tighter together.

Holding my hands up, I address them all.

"You don't have to be afraid of us. We're here to help. I have a van coming to take you anywhere you want to go. To the hospital, to a phone to call your family and those who may be interested, we have safe houses for women who have come from bad places such as this that you can stay at. We'll help you with food, a roof over your head and those who are ready, and a job."

I take a breath and look around the room waiting for one of them to speak.

One girl stands up, shielding all the others behind her although she looks to be the youngest. Probably only around fourteen.

"How do we know we can trust you?" She asks defiantly.

"At this very moment, I can't really answer that other than to say seeing is believing." I shrug, having answered honestly.

Her face pops into a small grin.

"Then let's go." Looking back at the ones behind her, she says, "We already thought we were going to die. What's worse than that?"

The rest of her group stands up with her. I hold in my grin at the guts this kid has.

Walking out they all follow behind, holding each other's hands with the girl being the leader. She holds her head up high as she walks past the rest of my men.

They all gasp, stopping briefly when we walk past where Animal is tied to a chair with his hands bleeding but none of them say a word.

Once outside, I check in with Buzz about Katrina and where the prospect is that is bringing the van to transport all these girls.

He tells me that Katrina is in my bed already sound asleep and that the prospect should be pulling up any minute.

"So about these safe houses. Are they just for the older women or can fifteen year old's go there too?" I hear a voice at my back and turn to find the young girl addressing me.

"Do you not have a family you want to go back to?" I ask gently.

"Nah. My mom sold me for meth when I was ten and I've been on the streets ever since." She shrugs. "So do you allow teenagers?"

"What's your name kid?" I ask her instead.

"Spawn."

"What kind of name is that?" I ask, looking at her to see if she's fucking with me.

She shrugs her shoulders. "It's the only name my mom ever called me. I don't know what my birth name is."

"Well I'm Skeeter. President of the Night Howler's MC."

"What's an MC?" Her brow wrinkles.

"It stands for Motorcycle Club."

"That is so cool! I like bikes." She grins widely and I just shake my head. "So, can I stay?" She asks just as the new van pulls up to the house.

"Yeah, Squirt, you can stay." I answer.

"Why you call me Squirt?" She demands.

"Because I am refusing right this minute to ever call you Spawn and because you are a little short for a fifteen year old."

She grins yet again. "Thanks."

"No problem. If you don't mind, could you help get the others in the van?" I ask her.

She runs off to do just that. How in the world her own mother could have treated her in such a way is beyond me.

Hell, I've known some mothers messed up on drugs that still loved their children.

I guess not everyone is meant to be a parent. If I had a little girl, I'd spoil her every chance that I got.

I watch as the van finally leaves ten minutes later. Grabbing my bag, I head into the house.

"Everyone out." I order and everyone leaves without comment.

"Big bad Prez. You going to shoot me?" Animal says through gritted teeth.

"Nope." I say calmly, pulling out my large handheld hatchet with razor sharp saw like teeth that was issued to me while in the service.

His eyes enlarge as I stand up, walking closer to him.

Grabbing one of his hands untying it, I pull it across the table. He tries to pull back but I'm stronger than he is.

Holding his wrist down so that his fingers are splayed out straight, I bring my hatchet down chopping his fingers off.

His screams are drowned out by the rage that is now front and center of my brain.

I smile as I watch blood squirting from the ends of where his fingers just were.

"You fucker! You chopped off my fucking fingers!"

Smiling at him, I push his shirt up and push my hatchet into his stomach on one side. Bringing it straight across, opening his insides.

I cut all the other ties holding him to the chair then dig my hand into his stomach grabbing his intestines. Pulling it out in one long string.

He continues screaming but is getting quieter by the second as he bleeds out.

Before the last of his insides are on the ground in front of him, he takes his last breath.

Getting up, I walk over to the sink and clean my hands as well as my hatchet.

Looking back at the asshole one last time, I grab my bag and walk out the door. Some of my guys are waiting for me just a few feet from the porch.

"Burn it to the ground." I say, walking back towards my bike.

I'm ready to see my girl. The rage inside of me once again quieted for now.

Chapter 11
Katrina

As soon as we get to Skeeter's house, Buzz tries to get me to eat something but instead I go to his bedroom and lay down.

I feel completely exhausted although I don't fall asleep quickly.

Instead my brain goes nuts with worry about why Skeeter didn't want me to stay with him.

Does he think that Animal had my body so now he doesn't want me anymore?

I know that I'm probably being crazy about all of this but I can't help it. He and I were just growing closer before I was taken yet again.

Still feeling dirty and the dried blood on my wrists pulling at my skin, I get up and go through Skeeter's things to find something to change into.

Once inside the bathroom, I turn the water on as hot as I can stand it, stepping under the spray with all my clothes still on.

As I stand there, I think of my sister and the tears once again begin to fall. I failed her all those months ago when I didn't force her to leave with me and I failed her again by not helping the law capture the man that killed her.

He's still out there somewhere, breathing the air that my sister should have been breathing instead of him.

One day, he will be found and I will make certain that he never breathes again.

Feeling a little better, I strip off my dirty clothes, leaving them in the bottom of the shower and scrub my skin until its red.

Although Animal didn't touch me more than what he did, I still feel gross from the thoughts of what could have happened.

Once I feel completely clean again, I get out and dress in one of Skeeter's large shirts. Walking back into the bedroom, I crawl between the sheets and close my eyes.

Skeeter

I park my bike right in front of the porch just as Buzz comes out of the house.

"She still asleep?" I ask.

"Yeah. I tried to fix her something to eat right after we got here but she refused."

"I'll make sure she eats. I'm sure that stupid fuck didn't feed her much, if at all." I growl.

"I'm going to head over to the clubhouse and try to help get some of the girls settled for the night before I head home." He says, walking over to his bike.

"Thanks man. Oh, one of the girls isn't but fifteen. Put her in the room next door to mine in the clubhouse."

"What? Why?" He looks at me like I've lost my mind.

"Because she's just a kid and I don't want her around some of those women we have in the safe houses."

"That makes sense." He chuckles, remembering that some of those women are straight up whores. "What's her name?" He asks.

"All she remembers her mom calling her is Spawn, but I call her Squirt. And do me another favor. See if you can get any more details from her about where she may have come from. We need to know what her birth name is."

"You got it." He nods, starting up his bike as I walk into the house.

Going to the lock box in the extra bedroom, I open it and place my bag down inside of it before locking it back.

Walking over to my bedroom, I open the door slowly and see that Katrina left the bedside lamp on. She's probably afraid of the dark.

Looking down at myself I decide to get a shower before lying down with her. Quietly walking into the bathroom, I shut the door and hop into the shower washing myself quickly of all the shit from early tonight.

Drying off, I don't bother with any clothes, going straight to the bed and climbing in, pulling Katrina back into my arms.

She wakes up startled.

"Sorry. It's just me." I whisper.

She smiles softly back, wrapping herself around me. Closing my own eyes, I fall asleep holding her as tightly as I can without hurting her.

Katrina

I wake up with a start and look around the room, afraid that I'm still in the house with Animal.

Remembering that Skeeter came for me and that this is his room, I wonder where he is until I hear someone in the kitchen.

Getting up, I slip on a pair of his sweatpants and walk towards the sounds of pans clattering together.

Peeping around the door into the kitchen, I see Skeeter standing at the stove cooking.

The smell of bacon, eggs and even toast hits my senses making my stomach growl so loud that Skeeter's head swivels my way.

"Good morning." He says with a smile and I walk further into the room.

"Morning." I answer, unsure how he currently feels about me.

"I was just about to come wake you. Take a seat, its ready now. Do you want coffee, milk or water?" He looks at me.

"Um, do you have a creamer?"

"That I do not have but I'll be sure to put it on the list for next time." He grins.

"I'll just have water then." I answer, sitting down at the table.

A few seconds later, he sets a plate in front of me before going back for his own and sitting in the chair across from me.

I eat slowly, not really looking up from my plate.

"I borrowed some clothes. Hope you don't mind." I say.

"Not at all. I think they look better on you anyway."

His comment makes me blush, my entire face turning red. My eyes jump up to him when I feel his fingers on my cheek.

"I love it when you do that." He whispers.

"Do what?"

"Turn bright red when I compliment you. It's sexy as hell."

My face heats yet again as he chuckles.

"You need to finish eating. I doubt you've had much the last few days and Buzz said you didn't eat last night."

"My stomach's in knots." I admit.

"Why? You're safe here with me. No one will ever hurt you again. I swear it."

"It's not that."

"Then what is it?" He asks.

My hands fidget with the shirt I'm wearing.

"I remember everything now. About what happened with my sister, the trial, and witness protection, all of it."

"Yeah. I'm sorry you had to go through that with Julie."

I look up quickly at him.

"You know about Julie?" I ask, wondering how long he's known.

"I found out yesterday. Buzz was able to find all the case files. Plus an Agent Newman called me." His mouth forms a tight thin line.

Remembering the Agent who swore that I would be safe, anger floods my own veins.

"I'm not going back into witness protection!" I burst out and Skeeter chuckles at me.

"No, you're not. I can't trust those bastards to keep you safe. Especially when he all but admitted to me they knew who you were after we found you in that warehouse but did nothing to help you."

"I'm not sure if I feel safe at the safe house either." I admit.

"I was hoping you'd stay with me."

Looking into his face, I see that he's being sincere but is he asking because he truly cares about me or because he just wants to make sure that I am safe. In my mind there is a difference.

"Why?" I ask.

"Why what?"

"Why do you want me to stay with you? Is it just because someone might be after me?"

My heart jumps in my chest rapidly, afraid that is exactly his reason why.

He pushes his seat away from the table and I think he's going to walk away. Instead he kneels next to me, turning my chair so that I'm facing him.

"I want you with me because I want you there. Not just because you are a woman in need of protection, even though you are. I want to feel you next to me while I sleep and wake up to your kiss every morning. The question is whether you want that too or not?"

Tears fill my eyes as I look at him.

This man that has saved me more than once is actually afraid that I don't want him. How stupid is that?

He smiles broadly at me and I wonder if I accidentally said that out loud.

Reaching my own hand up, I cup the side of his face.

"I want to stay with you." I whisper back.

He pulls me down to his lips and I more than eagerly accept his kiss.

His hands skim up my sides, slipping inside the shirt and cupping my bare breasts.

My nipples peak at the touch and I moan into his mouth. He becomes a mad man after that as my shirt flies over my head and he throws it down, covering my nipple with his mouth.

"Oh." I moan again, grabbing the back of his head as he sucks even harder.

My center throbs and I squirm on the seat.

His hands move to the waistband of the sweats, pulling them down.

I have to lift up slightly for him to get them down to my knees.

His mouth leaves my nipple, heading down across my stomach.

His beard tickling a path all the way to my clit.

Not taking any time at all, he sucks me into his hot mouth and if he hadn't been holding me in the seat, I'd have jumped out of it.

"Holy shit." I breathe out, enjoying his mouth as his tongue flicks my clit rapidly at the same time he's sucking hard.

I feel it building deep inside of me, my face flushing, my toes tingling with the sensation.

His fingers push up my thigh until I feel them at my slick opening and he pushes inside.

That's all the pressure I needed to jump over that ledge and I scream out my pleasure. The sound vibrating throughout the house.

It takes several minutes to come down from that high and I look down into his smiling eyes.

With me watching him, he pulls his fingers free and licks them clean.

"Holy shit." I whisper once again.

"Yeah. Holy shit." He chuckles.

Chapter 12

3 Years Later

Tanker

Looking around the courthouse lawn, there are bikers everywhere.

Although they won't let any of us in as it's a closed courtroom, we are all here in support of Skeeter's wife, Katrina.

It took them two more years with help from us to track down the guy responsible for the trafficking ring that held Katrina and a lot of other girls for so long.

I hear laughing behind me and I turn to see Squirt, Skeeter and Katrina's adopted daughter playing cards with several of the guys.

She's apparently beating their asses at poker, judging by the mountain of crackers they are using as poker chips.

"Jesus, that kid has skill." Reaper, the Prez of our mother chapter of the Night Howler's says from beside me. "Skeeter teach her?" He asks.

"Nope. She was that good when she first came to live at the clubhouse. She's extremely smart too. They took her for an evaluation a few weeks ago. Doctors said she was on the genius level or some shit."

"That's awesome. Maybe she'll be a doctor or something one day." He says just as the game ends and Squirt looks our way.

"A doctor? Hell no!" She exclaims and I chuckle at her expression knowing what she's about to say.

"What you going to go to school for?" Reaper asks her, truly interested.

"I'm not. Going to school that is. Why waste my money on something that I can learn from reading a book." She rolls her eyes.

Reaper looks over at me and I whisper, "Photographic memory too." His eyes widen.

"Go ahead and tell him what your plans are, Squirt." I say to her.

"I'm going into the military just like my daddy did only; I want to be a Navy Seal." She announces proudly.

"A girl? As a Seal?" One of the other guys asks loudly.

Her eyes narrow into slits as she looks his way.

"You think I can't do it?"

"I'm not saying you can't." He holds his hands up in submission. "It's just, I've never heard of a female Seal before." He shrugs.

"Well the Navy has finally opened it up where we women can try out. Just because you are men doesn't mean you are more special than women." Her lip curls up in derision. "I'll not only be a Navy Seal but I'll be one of the greatest snipers ever known."

With that, she takes her crackers, stomping her way to where Buzz and his Ole lady are sitting at another table.

"Skeeter is going to have his hands full with that one." Reaper laughs out.

"He already does, brother."

At that moment, people begin filing out of the courthouse and the reporter's rush forward firing questions to everyone walking out.

All the bikers move as one and push between the reporters and the witnesses, ushering them to their cars.

Several bikers cover Skeeter and Katrina, not wanting them to be knocked around since Katrina is currently in her third trimester of pregnancy.

Getting her into the jeep, I looked at Skeeter.

"How'd it go?" I ask quickly.

He smiles deeply, "She did great. He'll never see outside a prison again."

I smile too as Skeeter hops into the driver seat. Once they take off, I jump on my own biker as well as all the other brothers and we ride hard back towards the club.

Parking my bike, I watch as Skeeter helps his wife out of the vehicle and as usually happens, I feel a pain as if something is missing from my life.

Maybe one day I'll find that special someone that I feel the need to always keep close to me and protect.

For now, I'll help my married brothers protect what's theirs.

Nicole

"Hey Courtney, can you get me the file on the Lake Property outside of town please?"

My receptionist jumps at my voice. She's fairly new so she's still nervous about messing up but she came highly recommended by a family friend.

"Here you go Mrs. Sage." She says and I just smile at her.

"I told you that it's more than fine for you to call my Nicole. Okay?"

"Yes, ma'am." She rushes back to her desk to answer the phone.

Looking through the file, I familiarize myself once again with the whole property. I'm meeting a client there shortly that is looking to buy the entire one hundred sixty acres.

I have been wondering why he's interested in it. From what I know about him, he's the President of a local motorcycle club and while I will say I don't know much about that lifestyle, I know what I hear on the news.

"Mrs...I mean Nicole?"

"What is it?" I look up at Courtney.

"That was Mr. Reaper. He said that he couldn't make it today but that he was sending his wife and a friend of his to walk the property with you if that was okay."

My brow furrows. "How will I know if he wants it if he doesn't look at it?" I sit back in my chair in a huff.

"He said that his wife will be the final decision maker on whether or not the club adds it to their portfolio."

She raises her brow and I laugh too because since when does a motorcycle club have a portfolio?

Looking down at my watch, I notice that I have only enough time to get through the city streets and there before the appointed time to meet.

"Thank you Courtney. You can go home as soon as you finish the filing. Make sure you lock up."

Grabbing my papers, I stuff them into my case and run out the door.

Twenty minutes later, I'm right on time as another vehicle pulls up behind me at the Lake Property outside of town.

I don't pay attention to the people getting out of the jeep as I pull my briefcase out, shutting my door.

Turning around, I see a very beautiful woman walking towards me with her hand out.

"Hello. I'm Katrina, Skeeter's wife. He said he'd let you know I'd be here."

"Oh, yes, of course. It's nice to meet you. I'm Nicole Sage."

She smiles then turns to the man next to her that I hadn't yet looked at. When I do finally look up at him, I'm jolted by his mere size.

He holds his hand out and I automatically shake it as well but I expect him to squeeze too hard. Instead, he holds my hand in his gently.

"This is Tanker." Katrina says by way of introduction.

"Jesus, you're big." I whisper unexpectedly and turn every shade of red as his smile widens.

A jolt runs up my arm from where our hands are connected.

"So I've been told." He answers, letting go of my hand.

Getting control of myself once again, I turn to Katrina with a smile.

"Shall we?" I turn towards the building in front of us and try not to watch the sexy as sin Tanker out the corner of my eye.

THANK YOU FOR BEING such a loyal fan! To stay up to date with upcoming releases, follow me on social media!

Fang's Miracle

Wolfsbane Ridge MC

Book 7

Chapter 1

Fang

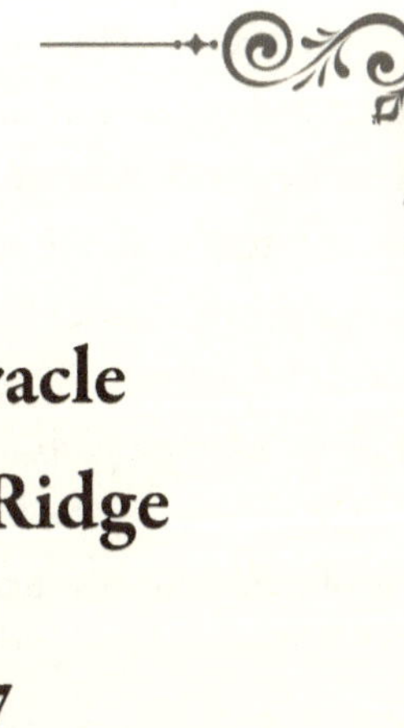

The clubhouse is busy today with the preparations for Thanksgiving dinner tomorrow at the hospital. Our VP's ole lady started a tradition last year of cooking for the families staying in the children's wing.

"Okay, now that everyone is here, Mina has an announcement to make." Prez speaks loudly to get everyone's attention.

Looking over at his ole lady, I wait to see what is going on. This is obviously not a regular Church meeting because the women are never included in those.

"We are planning to do a secret Santa for the kids at the hospital this year. Tomorrow after all the kids and their families eat dinner, we will each draw names from a bowl. Whoever's name you draw will be who you need to buy gifts for." She looks at the crowd of faces until she stops at mine. "Real gifts Fang."

I smile lopsidedly at her, not saying a word. She already knows me too well. Although I still haven't gotten even with her and the other girls for the frog fiasco a few years back when I was still a prospect. I've gotta admit it was pretty fucking epic what those women planned and executed.

"Don't forget that everyone needs to be on time tomorrow. Those of you that are helping get the food there need to be at Bella's Brew no later than ten a.m. The rest of you should be here to ride to the hospital in formation." Prez says before calling the impromptu meeting to a close.

Walking over to the bar, I spot Dane sitting on a stool with a beer in his hand.

"Getting started kind of early, huh?" I say, taking the seat next to him.

He shrugs his shoulders, "It's five o'clock somewhere."

Signaling to the prospect manning the bar to bring me a cold one, I look back at Dane. He seems to be lost in thought more and more these days.

I've known him for a long time so I know the holidays are a huge problem for him. He's never told me all the details; I just know it has something to do with his family that live back East. Although this year he seems a little worse for wear.

"You okay, man?" I finally break the silence.

"Just been thinking a lot. About family and shit." He looks around the room at the other brothers.

Order Today!
https://books2read.com/FangsMiracle

Marissa Ann spends her time in rural North Mississippi with her husband, the kids and all of their animals on a hobby farm.

She always said she would write books one day even though many thought she never would. She made a promise to a childhood friend who left this world for the next in 2015. That she would finally write and publish at least one.

Her first book hit the market in 2018 and she's never looked back. She now has several out with many more scheduled for release. Want to stay up to date with new releases, giveaways and all the cool things? **Sign up for Marissa's newsletter here**[1] or join **Marissa Ann Romance Readers**[2] on Facebook.

Join Marissa Online

WEBSITE:
www.authormarissaann.com[3]
Facebook:
https://www.facebook.com/MarissaAnnAuthor
Instagram:
https://www.instagram.com/authormarissaann/
Twitter:
https://twitter.com/marissaannbooks
Goodreads:
https://www.goodreads.com/author/show/18159855.Marissa_Ann
Linkedin:
https://www.linkedin.com/in/marissa-ann-ballard-93982b186/
Tik Tok
https://www.tiktok.com/@authormarissaann
Bookbub:

---

1.   **https://www.authormarissaann.com/**

2.   **https://www.facebook.com/groups/1543661216008591/**

3.   http://www.authormarissaann.com

https://www.bookbub.com/profile/marissa-ann

Read More of Marissa's Books

BOOK 1 TIMBER'S FAIRY
   https://books2read.com/TimbersFairy
Book 2 Blade's Pixie
   https://books2read.com/BladesPixie
Book 3 Blood's Angel
   https://books2read.com/BloodsAngel
Book 4 Wrench's Salvation
   https://books2read.com/WrenchsSalvation
Book 5 Bear's Saviour
   https://books2read.com/BearsSaviour
Book 6 Torque's Gaze
   https://books2read.com/TorquesGaze
Fang's Miracle
   https://books2read.com/FangsMiracle
Night Howler's MC, Mississippi
Book 1 Reaper's Jewels
   https://books2read.com/ReapersJewels
Book 2 Grease
   https://books2read.com/Grease
Night Howler's MC Series, New Orleans
Book 1 Buzz
   https://books2read.com/BuzzNewOrleans
Book 2 Skeeter
   https://books2read.com/Skeeter
Giovanni's Obsession
   https://books2read.com/GiovannisObsession
All I've Got

https://books2read.com/AllIveGot
Poison Pen Series
Book 1 Baratta's Darkness
https://books2read.com/BarattasDarkness
Book 2 Lily's Shadow
https://books2read.com/LilysShadow
Book 3 Arin's Light
https://books2read.com/ArinsLight
Book 4 Mika's Heart
https://books2read.com/MikasHeart
Book 5 Cass' Vow
https://books2read.com/CassVow
Book 6 Shelby's Secret
https://books2read.com/ShelbysSecret

www.ingramcontent.com/pod-product-compliance
Lightning Source LLC
Chambersburg PA
CBHW031002210726
48290CB00007B/2430